A Man Jumps Out of an Airplane

Stories by Barry Yourgrau

CLARKSON POTTER/PUBLISHERS
NEW YORK

A Man Jumps Out of an Air-plane

Some of these pieces have appeared in a chapbook by Whale Cloth Press, and in the following publications: *The Paris Review, The New York Times, Bomb, Washington Review of the Arts, Hanging Loose, Appearances, kayak, The World, Telephone, The Poetry Project Newsletter, East Village Eye, Joe Soap's Canoe, Scholastic Magazine* and *Dumb Magazine.* "Apocrypha" appeared in *Poetry.* 𝔇 The author would like to thank the New York State Council on the Arts for a Creative Artists Public Service Fellowship in Fiction, and the Ragdale Foundation for its generous hospitality. The author would also like to express his gratitude to Paul Violi and to Marian Young.

Published by Clarkson N. Potter, Inc., 201 East 50th Street, New York, New York 10022. Member of the Crown Publishing Group. Originally published by SUN in 1984.
CLARKSON N. POTTER, POTTER and colophon are trademarks of Clarkson N. Potter, Inc.

Manufactured in the United States of America

Book design by Jane Treuhaft

LIBRARY OF CONGRESS CATALOGING-IN-PUBLICATION DATA
Yourgrau, Barry.
    A man jumps out of an airplane / Barry Yourgrau.
        p.   cm.
    I. Title.
    PS3575.O94M3   1992
    813'.54—dc20   91-19291
                                                          CIP

ISBN 0-517-58717-3
10 9 8 7 6 5 4 3 2 1
FIRST CLARKSON N. POTTER EDITION

For

my

parents,

and

for

Matt

THE THOUGHTS THAT WE CAN CLEARLY GRASP
ARE VERY LITTLE THOUGHTS . . .
ALL GREATER THOUGHTS ARE UNDEFINED AND VAST
TO OUR POOR CHILDISH BRAINS.

Jerome K. Jerome
Idle Thoughts
of An Idle Fellow

Milk · 1   Village Life · 2   Snow · 3

Femme Fatale · 4   Scenery · 5

Travelogue · 6   Apocrypha · 8

Journey · 9   Song · 10   Out of Water · 11

Hula Horror · 12   Memento Mori · 14

Cuckoo Clock · 15   Demoiselle · 16

Helium · 18   The Joke · 19

The Shipwreck · 20   The Wonders · 21

Primavera · 22   Natural Law · 23   Warts · 24

Djin · 25   Fried Clams · 26   Texas · 27

In the Meadow · 28   The Surprise · 29

From Childhood · 31   Zoology · 32

Creek · 33   Fog · 34   Aquarium · 36

Nursery Tale · 37   Far Region · 38

On the Lake · 39   Bones · 40   Garden · 41

Domestic Farce · 42   Katzenjammer · 43

De Maupassant · 48   Ars Poetica · 50

Con

Horse Opera · 51   Three-Ring Circus · 52

Origins · 53   Honky-Tonk · 55

Soup Bone · 57   Strawberries · 58

Little Fire · 60   Moon and Ladder · 61

From a Book of Hours · 62

Two Bears · 63   Golden Years · 65

Talk · 66   Tired Magician · 68

Call of Nature · 69   Horror Movie · 70

Full Moon · 71   Big Red Nose · 73

Sport · 74   My Father · 76

Renovation · 77   Sheep · 79   Angels · 80

Bomb · 81   Evening · 82

In the Ice Age · 83   Hermione · 84

Greenland · 85   Snot · 86   Mask · 87

Blood · 89   The Cousin · 90

The Greek · 92   Dummy · 94   Lattice · 95

Box · 96   Woodsmen · 97

tents

A Man Jumps Out of an Airplane

Milk

ON A BET, A MAN CLIMBS INSIDE A COW. ONCE THERE he decides to stay. The cow's interior is warm and soft, although very dark. But the man's eyes get by with the driblets of light that do manage to seep in. Food is no problem: there's milk and more milk. "Fresher than dairy-fresh," the man wisecracks to himself, chuckling, as he pulls off his socks. No need for clothes, after all, so why bother keeping them on? He bundles them up and stuffs them down the appropriate cavity, thinking slyly of how they'll end up.

Then he lies back and dozes. The movements of the cow, now that she's quieted down, are lulling. The man's friends are still out there, beside themselves: every once in a while they band their hoarse voices into a collective shriek of protest—protest from the world of sanity and reality. But their cries grow hoarser and feebler, and then disappear altogether into the milky stomach mucus with which the man loads up his ears. Slowly, with the contented grace of a baby, he falls into a deep sleep.

Outside the sun creeps away and the moon climbs up over the pasture. The cow wanders slowly, still cautious in her gait, chewing cud. Finally she sinks with heavy care onto the grass, well away from the rest of the herd. Her large, sensitive eyes brim with concern as she tries to fathom her new fate and responsibility. ☙

Village Life

COUNTRY GIRLS, RED-CHEEKED AND BUXOM, STAND FEET wide apart at a counter. They lean on it, elbows propped, forearms crossed. They chat. Their skirts are gathered above their waists.

An old man plods down the line of them with a bucket. He reaches in between the thighs of each girl and puts the fruit he brings out into the bucket. The girls laugh. The atmosphere is easy. They mock the old man, they make cracks and someone ruffles his few hairs.

The old man's tired, stolid expression never changes. When he has finished with the line, he has three buckets of fruit. The girls shake down their skirts, sighing and chuckling.

The old fellow carries the buckets by yoke out to an open shed. He cleans a couple of clay bowls with the sleeve of his jacket. The fruit tumbles from the buckets into the bowls. The old man hangs a blanket across the mouth of the shed. He blows his nose in a big, dirty handkerchief.

By suppertime, the line already stretches a long way back among the houses. It's Saturday night. The young men of the village are fresh-shaven, their simple dark jackets are brushed and buttoned, their hats set carefully on their damp, odorous heads. They fidget, staring anxiously towards the shed. The one at the front of the line pays for his ticket from the snuffling old man and steps quickly into the darkness behind the blanket. After a while— sometimes a short while, sometimes a long while—the youth comes out. Wiping clumsily at his mouth, he hurries, grinning, towards his waiting friends. ⋑

Snow

I GO TO THE TRAIN STATION TO MEET MY GIRLFRIEND.
I am wearing all kinds of scarves against the weather. It is snowing. The train comes in but my girlfriend isn't on it. A conductor
covered with snowballs informs me that my girlfriend has had
plastic surgery without telling me, and the operation got fouled
up, and now she's too ashamed ever to see me again.

I go home, a multitude of ambivalences battling within me. I
keep peering about for anyone swathed in bandages, in case she
might have come out here secretly on the bus.

At home, I remember the telephone in the freezer. I take it
out. The surface of the receiver is brown and wilted, like old
lettuce. But the inside will probably still be good. "She can use
this to graft with," I think. I turn on the tap in the sink and begin
carefully scraping off the outside of the receiver. The phone rings
in my hands. I don't answer it, I want to surprise her. The ringing
goes on a long time before stopping. I start to feel guilty. What if
she really needed me? I lose heart with the surprise and finally
wreck the good stuff by accidentally tearing off a piece.

I go into the bathroom and begin tying knots in the scarves, out
of despair. There is a knock at the front door. The train conductor comes in, dripping, and says, "Didn't you recognize me?" ☽

Femme Fatale

I HAVE THE LAST PACK OF CIGARETTES IN THE WORLD; but no matches. I am in the bedroom, which has an enormous window, so I have to keep my body between the cigarettes and the window. Everybody is in the other room with the matches. I try to think of some disguised way of asking for the matches without giving away my secret.

I can't think of any. I go out into the other room, hang around for a while in a state of desperate appetite, then sneak downstairs and open the broom closet, releasing the bull. I rush back upstairs and tell everybody that the bull is loose!

They all go downstairs, except for one blonde. To keep her ignorant of my real interests, I seduce her. She tells me she is so glad someone is finally seducing her, because she has just been fired from her job. After we have necked a bit, I suggest she go to the bathroom and prepare herself. She goes off coquettishly, saying she will tell me later all about why she *really* lost her job.

Immediately I rifle through the handbags that are lying around, find some matches and run into my room. But before I can light up I hear her coming out of the bathroom. I hide the matches and cigarettes. We start to fuck. I am unhappy; as I feel myself coming I moan "No! No!" because I don't want to come, I want to smoke.

Suddenly there is cigarette smoke streaming from her mouth and her fingernails are on fire. I snap into a terrific ecstasy. ⅅ

Scenery

MY FATHER TAKES ME INTO A DORMITORY WHERE THERE are hundreds of figures sleeping in beds. "Isn't this wonderful!" he whispers. "Yeah," I agree, although privately I think, "Big deal, what's so terrific about a lot of people sleeping?"

Outside, there is a huge walled garden. We walk among the moonlit flowers. My father still can't get over what we've seen inside. "Have you ever seen anything like it?" he cries. I make some vague movement with my head. His enthusiasm is really bugging me. "What about this garden?" I think. "This is what's sensational: the paths and statues; the moonlight and shadows; the aromas." We walk along, the gravel crunching underfoot in the silence. Abruptly my father halts. I immediately think it's to rest on account of his back or any one of the histrionic multitude of ailments which enable him to use a cane and make a scene whenever he wants. But instead he grabs my arm and says, "It was such a wonderful sight, let's go back and have another look!" I gape at him, unbelieving, horrified. "You really want to?" I ask. "Yes!" he says, squeezing my arm, putting on his wonderfully-impulsive-guy, life-with-a-capital-L look. "Don't you?" I smile weakly. "Okay," I tell him, shrugging, "sure, if you'd like to." We plod back. I can't believe what we're doing, I want to weep with the absurdity of it. The garden beckons like a medieval fantasy. We leave it and come back into the cold hall. It's like an auditorium. From where we stand the beds go into the distance for fifty yards. My father nudges me, beaming, his eyes misty with tears. ✺

Travelogue

I HAVE A BAD SCALP CONDITION. I GO TO THE DOCTOR. In her office, she hands me a brochure and starts to talk. At first I am thoroughly confused by her terminology; then I realize, looking at the posters on the walls, that I am in a travel bureau. The doctor is very enthusiastic about the country she is selling me on: it has lice perhaps as big as my thumb, she says, and there is no fresh meat available whatsoever. "So you think this scalp thing might have something to do with *diet?*" I ask, straining earnestly to follow her line of diagnosis.

She stares at me, blinking in puzzlement. Then she shakes her head a couple of times, as if to clear it, and rolls her shoulders, and begins poking through some brochures. Finally she pulls one out. "Okay!" she says. "Here's a country where the weather is usually pretty awful right around the time of your trip, and everything is incredibly expensive."

I look at her, trying to translate her remarks into plain language, trying to find any kind of diagnosis camouflaged among the lines. I can't. I notice, really for the first time, that she is wearing only a bikini and that she considers me through the panes of enormous circular sunglasses, like some species of disco owl. "You're a funny kind of doctor," I tell her, and I get up to leave.

On the way out, I pass by a pool. Bathing beauties lounge on its tiled shores, sipping drinks from pineapples through glittering straws. I step towards them, then I remember the disfiguring condition of my scalp. I catch myself and scuttle woefully out the door.

At home I sit in the fusty dimness of the living room, fingering my head. "She didn't know a lot about medicine," I think, "but I'll bet she knows a lot about other kinds of things." I doze off. In my dream we are on a desert island. I have managed to get her to take off her bikini. I wear the bra part on my head,

Mouseketeer/babushka style. "So you really think this will work?" I ask her. She looks up from her ukelele and smiles tenderly. "Not a chance," she tells me. ✑

Apocrypha

A MAN IS FISHING IN AN UNFAMILIAR CREEK. HE LOOKS over and sees a baby come bobbing around the bend. The baby is in a kind of wicker basket.

The man drops his rod and splashes in hurriedly up to his waist and scoops the kid up before he drifts off into the distance and God knows what harm. He brings the peculiar, dripping burden up onto the bank.

He sits there, bewilderedly dabbing his handkerchief at the kid's cheeks. The little one seems okay despite his ordeal. He has on a little loincloth. The man touches it. He whistles: it sure seems to be gold. He looks around. Whoever was taking care of the kid is nowhere in sight. The man gets up and goes to the top of the bank and peers over the bushes.

A spear appears in midair. It goes right through the man's head. The corpse reels dramatically down the bank and crashes spread-eagled with a mighty splash into the creek. Very slowly it spins and starts to float downstream, the shaft of the spear sticking up like a mast.

The baby starts bawling. The bushes at the top of the bank part and a dark, sullen face wearing a plumed helmet looks down.

At home, the dead man's wife hears the clock chiming. It gives her a start. She closes her Bible with a clap and hurries out to the kitchen to get dinner into the oven. She realizes to her shame how badly she had the story jumbled, and she feels a strange and mounting distress as she glances out at the empty driveway. ❧

Journey

A MAN MAKES A LITTLE PROSCENIUM IN A LIVING ROOM. He looks around over his shoulder. Then he climbs through. His new surroundings are miniature and picturesque. Snow is falling. He opens a big, dark, high-domed umbrella. He starts up the cobblestones beside a canal. A green barge toots mournfully as it passes: the snowflakes make a cap on its stern lamp. The man waves after it. He quickens his pace. In the silence he is aware of his breathing—the clouds of his breath—of the sounds of his footfall, the rub of his clothing, the minuscule patter of the falling snow.

He hurries along under his umbrella, beside the canal, until he is a small dark point, until he is indistinguishable in the silent scenery.

Later, someone comes into the room, and, going by the table to get a book, draws shut the toy-sized curtain. ꙮ

Song

For Tony Towle

A MAN GETS LOST IN A STORM AND WANDERS INTO A strange bar. He takes his drink to a table in a side room and watches the rain swirling down on the unfamiliar streets. He takes a pencil out of a pocket of his coat, finds a piece of paper in another and tries to draw a map of where he might be. But he can't figure it out: the map doesn't make any sense. He crosses it out. The wind rattles the windowpane roughly. The man leans his cheek on his hand and, idling, doodles a few choruses of a song he comes up with in his head. The results have something quite pleasing about them. Cheered, the man puts the paper away and goes back to the bar in the main room, for a refill. "Okay, I give up, where am I?" he says to the bartender, pretending good-naturedly to be exasperated. The bartender grins back over his shoulder from the ranks of glistening bottles. "That's a nice little lyric you got there," he says. The man draws back and looks at the bartender incredulously. The bartender presses a button, and just like that the rain stops. ♪

Out of Water

IT'S POURING. A GIRL IS AT A BUS STOP, SOAKED TO the skin. She looks like a student, judging from the batch of books under her arm. I tell her she'll catch pneumonia; she should come up to my place and dry off. She says thanks, she's okay, but I insist with gentlemanly concern. She hesitates; but finally, with a worried look, she yields.

Upstairs, she comes out of the bathroom in my robe drawn tight. She towels her dark, glossy hair. She's much lovelier than I'd realized, and I notice with a pang of tenderness that she still keeps on her funny green socks. It must be a custom in her native land—she's a foreigner, judging from her wonderfully liquid accent I can't place. I make her some tea and then I have to tell her that in spite of my genuinely honorable intentions I've fallen completely in love with her, what am I going to do? Her response is to sit with the cup between her hands, staring into her tea, her brow knotted in concentration. I realize she is actually trying to figure out what I should do—a real little scholar. I let out a laugh. "Don't worry," I tell her gently. "I know what to do."

I go around to the chair beside her and put my hand on her shoulder and kiss her tenderly on the cheek. I get a startlingly oily and fishy taste. It's so unexpected I can't stop myself from showing a look of shocked surprise. She sees it and blushes and bends deeper over her cup. She points a lovely hand at the wet books on the table. They're academic treatises on salt- and freshwater fish. "Those are my ancestors I'm studying," she murmurs. ૩

Hula Horror

IT'S VERY LATE AT NIGHT—VERY EARLY IN THE MORNing. I'm in a thatched-roof hut. Earthern floor. Kerosene lamp. A girl—a fellow tourist—has gotten drunk and is now dancing just for me, lasciviously as she can manage, in the middle of the place. She sways and bobs, come-hither style. She's stripped off her clothing and is attired solely in a "native" grass hula skirt, colored pink.

I drink, as I have copiously all evening; the gramophone squalls, the lamp throws a melodramatic light, harsh, utterly black in the shadows. I keep time with my glass, thinking, "Man, the brochures don't tell you about *this*," and then a horrible realization pops into my mind, like a window shade flying up. That pink skirt, I realize, my skin turning icy—that pink skirt is hideously *evil*: it's an instrument of black magic, a voodoo booby trap planted here on us two boozed-up, woollybrained tourists.

The girl of course is utterly ignorant of this. She's not exactly the brainy type to start with. I rise from my chair slowly, wideeyed, watching in horror as she runs her fingers teasingly through the waving mess of pink strands. I wave my hands for her to stop. "Don't!" I tell her. "Stop it!" My throat is all tightened up. She thinks I'm teasing. She giggles, yummily, wiggles her boobs at me and shimmies backwards, away from me, enticing. I go towards her. "You don't understand!" I whisper desperately. She squeezes her eyes shut for a second and laughs, all dimples. "Oh yup I do!" she gurgles.

I jump for her. She dodges me and goes scooting, squealing, out the door. I grab as she heads into the night and get a handful of pink grass. It writhes in my hands. Screaming soundlessly, I struggle with it on the floor. Frantically I flap behind me with one hand for something heavy. I get something—an individualportion casserole of our "native" dinner—and with it I pound and pound on the twitching strands, driving them into the earth, spraying Spanish rice all over the room.

I sprawl backwards, gasping. The air is full of drumbeats, pulsations. I crawl to the door. In the distance, surrounded by an unearthly, bizarre luminosity, the girl is doing her dance of the seven veils encircled by a ring of fat white candles in the undergrowth. She is sputtering with idiotic excitement, gleefully shouting for me, still absolutely unaware of the nightmare taking place, because she shakes her hips but she doesn't have to: the skirt is clearly moving of its own accord. I watch as it begins to climb up her ribs. She squeals ticklishly and slaps at it.

I can't bear to see what's coming. I scramble up and frantically throw some things into a suitcase. I heave it out the window and clamber after it. Perhaps she will divert attention long enough to cover my escape. I rush into the darkness. I can hear her screaming now. I try to go faster. The moon pops from behind a cloud, suddenly, as if a garish spotlight had been switched on, flooding the way as I plunge down through the ever-pinkening brush. 🐍

Memento Mori

A YOUNG MAN STANDS IN THE CURTAINS OF HIS BED-room window. Through binoculars he watches the funeral home across the street, where a crowd is arriving for a service. Sad young girls with bare legs emerge from limousines and file across the veranda in a somber promenade. Their sadness invades him, tears fill up the eyepieces of the binoculars and disturb the lenses. Diffractions of giant legs, bare and smooth-skinned, voluptuous, rise to the young man's eyes. Compassion and monstrous excitement struggle in him. One of the mourners stumbles on the steps, showing her thighs. The young man is overwhelmed, he loses his balance and topples backwards on to the bed, dragging the curtains with him.

The binoculars clatter to the floor. They metamorphose into a pair of gilt, high-heeled sandals, with morgue numbers scratched in the rhinestones. ᴆ

Cuckoo Clock

A MIDDLE-AGED MAN AND HIS WIFE ARE GOING AT IT in the deep quilts of their old brass bed. The big, red-cheeked guy rams it in from behind, driving his wife's blotchy, fleshy shoulders deep into the bedclothes. From down there, under her tangle of braids, come muffled grunts and shouts. Suddenly the twosome sprawl forward. The guy squeezes and clutches ferociously in his ecstatic throes. Through the window the sun splashes on the snow, on the Alps across the valley.

Afterwards, there is coffee made with cocoa and milk, and little steaming almond buns.

Then, still naked, the big guy pads over to his work table. He has on his green felt hat, he smokes his funny, carved pipe. He tinkers with a cuckoo clock in a shaft of sunlight. "Cuckoo! Cuckoo!"

Out in the kitchen, his wife hangs up the dish towel and gets out the wicker basket. She also is naked. She climbs sideways through the window and steps heavily into the basket of a small hot-air balloon. She casts loose, and the balloon lifts slowly upwards. When it comes level with the chimney, she ties off the lines, expertly. She hums a tune to herself as she leans out to take in the laundry, which hangs from pegs just below the clouds. ☻

Demoiselle

I'M IN BED WITH A GIRL WHOSE HEAD IS ON CROOKED. But I know in my heart that if I really do a thorough job on her, really ecstasize her in a way she's obviously never been before, she'll straighten out. I fling myself into the task with messianic relish. I foreplay with the controlled exquisiteness of a French aesthete; I lock horns with the steady languor of a Zen master, timeless and temperate; then suddenly I kick the whole thing into overdrive—a lumberjack in a brand-new Cadillac. Off we roar down the coast highway! The rose of our delight crashes over us, drenches us in a hot shower of petals. We roll apart in a daze, and immediately I grope for the cigarettes to celebrate. Her head is perfectly aligned now, just as I knew it would be. But unbelievably, her legs are backwards.

Peeved, I throw the cigarettes away and grab her again. There'll be no mistake this time! At the last minute I wheel her on top of me and make like an oil derrick, we reenact the discovery of oil. I gush, she swoons. I pull out from under her collapsed form, and gasping from exertion, I forage under the sheets. I check her heels, I check her ass, I sit back, panting and vindicated. Everything's pointing in the same direction. Including, I realize, her breasts. Her goddamned breasts are sticking out of the middle of her back! I sink to the pillows, glowering.

It goes like this all afternoon. When her breasts are right, her hands are wrong. When her hands are right, the cheeks of her ass snuggle up under her belly. Finally the parts of her body are in a hopeless tangle and I give up. I sprawl on the floor, utterly wrung out, stung to the very quick of my self-esteem.

She sits at the bureau, humming to herself as she combs out the long red banner of her hair with a grotesquely misplaced hand. She dabs a little extra brightness on her lips: a practiced fingertip brushes once, twice, just above the top knob of her spine, where her lips happen to be. I watch as she dresses, hasty and competent despite the jumble of anatomy—she has an appointment to keep. She comes over to me when she's done and contorts herself to press a hand to my cheek. "Thanks . . ." she smiles, and from what I can see of her face, she thinks to show by her smile how truly exquisite are her feelings. The smile section is limpid with satisfaction. "It was just utterly swell . . ." She might as well have said: "Better luck next time." I watch dismally as she strolls out, pausing at the door to throw back a tangled kiss, the unregenerate cubism of her body making a mockery of the grand tradition of my powers. ◺

Helium

I OPEN THE BOX AND TAKE OUT THE HEAVY, FOLDED
balloon and fix it up to the cannister of helium. The balloon
swells spasmodically. Then suddenly it finds its form and goes
taut and hurriedly I shut off the gas. It's in the shape of my father.
It's a terrific job and worth all the money. There it hovers, against
the ceiling, like an obese bumblebee. I get on the bed and tie a
line to one foot and pull it after me out the door.

Behind our house is a small park, with a round hill. There's a
blue sky, a few clouds and a breeze. I release the balloon and it
hurries out, bumping into the wind, until it's at the end of my
line. Delighted, I fiddle with the string and my old man dances
idiotically under the clouds.

At this point I become aware of shouting. I look, my mother
is hurrying up the hill towards me, gesturing angrily. "What are
you doing with your father!!" she cries. "Get him down!" I start
to laugh gleefully at her confusion, but then I'm brought up short
by the intensity of her passion. "Relax, mom, it's a balloon," I
explain to her as she reaches me. "You must be crazy," she
hisses. She grabs the line out of my hand and starts pulling.
"Mom, it's just a balloon!" I protest, but then I look and it really
is my old man up there above the treetops. My stomach turns
over. I can hear him cursing. "Hang on, hang on!" my mother
cries, fighting his weight and the wind. Suddenly a gust shoves
him into the very top of a tree. "Oh my god!" my mother cries.

I shrink back from her, horrified at what is happening. I can
hear the snapping and tearing in the branches as my father roars
and struggles, and my mother's shrieks, "Don't break the line,
don't break the line!" I put my fingers in my ears and turn and
flee down the hill. At the bottom I look back and my mother is
standing silhouetted at the top, wailing and imploring the sky
with outstretched arms as my father sails away, a clamorous,
wind-blown blob, up into the blue. ◑

The Joke

BY WAY OF A JOKE, A MAN PUTS ON A DISGUISE. HE goes to visit his mother. His mother is also in a jovial mood; she also is in disguise. Unprepared, both of them get a shock at the front door. Neither of them says anything about it through the afternoon visit, which is strained and cautious and overly courteous. Privately each of them thinks the other is well on the way to cracking up, given the get-up, the paint, the tufts of colored hair. Their hearts are heavy and sick when their customary TV show ends. It's with great unease that they look over at each other, that they finally rise to bid good-bye. As the mother watches her son go down the garden path, a tear bubbles along the humpy contour of her papier mâché nose; it is absorbed by a huge nostril. The man waves from the gate; behind his funhouse glasses, his eyes are misty. He walks all the way home, head bowed under its bobbing rubber antennae.

Nothing like this dismal, mysterious episode occurs again; but subtly it haunts their relationship for years to come. ⑤

The Shipwreck

For Steven Campbell

AFTER THE SHIP HAS GONE DOWN, THERE ARE FIVE OF us in the lifeboat. The captain plays a melancholy air on the concertina. The two fat bankers' wives put their heads together and snuffle into their furs. The night is a moist caravan of stars, and the young pharmacist and I stare out past the gunwales, our hearts tugging at our throats.

The captain ends his song and spreads his hands. He asks us to understand . . . "C'est une affaire d'Amour," he says, the romance of ships and seas. It was beyond him to change her mind, he just wanted us to know that. He doesn't blame her. . . .

A shoal of drowned men drifts by, the little flowerpots of their souls resting on their milky, tattooed chests. The captain blesses them in the language of sailors.

Then he rises and takes up a position in the bow of the boat. Fidgeting with his hat and primping the tassels of his white uniform, he gazes restlessly out to sea.

We follow his gaze to a spot in the waves. The waves break open there and an enormous conch shell bobs to the surface. There is a mother-of-pearl chair in it, draped with velvety seaweed.

The strange craft comes alongside us, propelled by glittering fins. We all turn fearfully to the captain. Without a word to us he clambers down into the shell and seats himself in the chair. He opens a parasol. He looks nervous. The shell moves off.

The women cry out and cross themselves on their bosoms. The pharmacist utters an oath. "Adieu! Adieu!" the captain calls softly. He waves to us with the dainty fingers of his hand. He blinks as the first foam splashes over him.

Soon there is no more of him, only the suggestion of music and the shadowy movement of lanterns under the sea. 🜚

The Wonders

I AM IN A GREAT HOUSE. I GO ALONG THE CORRIDOR. I open a door. A naked girl reclines against the pillows of a bed, her knees drawn up and open. A monkey squats before her. His paws are clasped together and raised, his grimacing face is lifted, towards heaven. It is the age-old attitude of supplication. The room is silent. A candle burns by the bedside, before the heavy curtains. The girl turns her head languorously to look at me in the doorway. On her face there is an expression of elegiac softness, a half-smile: languid, patient, tender.

I close the door quietly. I go down the corridor. "This place is full of wonders," I tell myself. I pause at the window, to look down at an apple tree in the yard below. Under its boughs, a bestiary has gathered to watch a girl bathing herself from a porcelain bowl. ☙

Primavera

I GO FOR A WALK AT NIGHT IN A SCHOOL YARD IN THE country. It's early spring. I come around the corner of one of the old wooden buildings, and this is what I see: a hurricane lamp hangs glowing from a tree. In its light a naked man is bent over a naked young girl whose head is in a metal washtub. At first I think, blushing, that they're doing some sex thing bobbing for apples, and I turn to go away; but then I see the guy is in fact holding down the girl's head in the tub: she squirms around, like she's choking.

I hurry towards them yelling. The guy turns around. He smiles as I come up. He's middle-aged and healthy-looking. He holds one hand on the girl's neck and gestures with the other. "It's a fertility rite," he explains pleasantly. "Are you kidding?" I tell him. The girl's hair is spread out in the water, and she squirms and grunts and paws softly at the grass. I reach out for his wrist to make him let go, and he gives a cry and tries to ward me off, and we get involved in an awkward, shifting, tugging struggle, made all the more bizarre there under the lamp by his nakedness. Finally we lose our balance together and sprawl violently over the girl and the tub, knocking everything all over the place.

I manage to pull free out of the tangle and get to my knees. The tub is upended on its side in front of an expanding, glistening pool; the girl droops in the grass, hacking, her skinny chest heaving. I stare at her, dumbfounded: with each watery cough of hers, the air fills with tiny fruits and flowers. They sift around her onto the grass, pale and stunted, a garden of puny litter.

"See what you've done?" the guy says. He sits next to me, rubbing his shoulder. He looks miserable. "Will you look at that measly stuff! Man," he groans, "don't you know *anything* about the seasons?" ⊅

Natural Law

A MAN GOES FISHING ON A WINDY DAY. NOTHING'S BIT-
ing, and the man starts home in the evening with an empty creel.
He stops off at a roadhouse for a drink. He brings his glass over
to a table and he notices a fish tank. He goes up to it: there are
a couple of gorgeous, stupid-looking trout inside. The man looks
at them and then looks over his shoulder. The bar is dim, and
empty but for a couple of locals busy with a bowl of peanuts at the
other end of the place.

It only takes a second for the man to slip a hand into the tank,
grab one fish then the other by the tail, lift them out, bash their
heads against the wall and drop them into the creel. He goes back
to his drink. He tosses it off and heads out to his car. No one tries
to stop him.

Back on the road, a feeling of unease, of moroseness, steals
over the man. Finally it gets so strong he pulls over. He sits for
a long time smoking a cigarette and looking at the creel. He feels
wretched: in spite of everything he is genuinely a fisherman at
heart.

He pushes the car door open and gets out dolefully under the
stars. He looks up at them: there must be millions. He kicks a
pebble back down towards the curve in the road and trudges in its
wake, lost in melancholy contemplation.

Back around the bend and down the road, a car without head-
lights bowls along. An out-of-season moose is strapped
figurehead-style to the hood: the great, bobbing sweep of the
antlers hangs forward like a razor-sharp, hugely pronged snow-
plow. A pair of drunken poachers are living it up at the dash-
board. They pelt each other with peanuts and hoot with laughter.
The driver is almost choking with merriment, ducking nuts as he
goes bursting into the dark curve. ℈

Warts

A FROG MAKES A NOISE UNDER A MAN'S WINDOW. THE man turns over and opens his eyes halfway long enough to grope by the bed for a shoe, which he heaves out of the window. Then he goes back to sleep.

The shoe hits the frog right on the side of its little head and knocks it flying in the midst of its nightly constitutional.

In retaliation it hops along the lawn to the hedge, gets up to the bedroom window by a series of vaulting maneuvers, hops stealthily onto the man's bed and empties its bladder all over the man's foot. Chuckling, it hops out the window and back to the lily pond.

In the morning, the man shambles out to the bathroom. He's all lathered up in the shower before he registers the condition of his foot: it's a mass of warts.

Out in the lily pond, the frog hears the screams. It croaks contentedly, grinning. It paddles over the pond's edge, to take everything in. Gloating, it gets up on the bank and puffs itself full of air and bellows noisily.

At this point a fat boy springs heavily out from behind a tree. Gleefully he pulls both triggers of his father's shotgun. There is a deafening blast. The boy comes plodding through the clouds of smoke to the bank. He peers at the great ragged cavity where the frog used to be. "Huh?" he says. "Where'd it go?" He sneers, baffled, into the smoke. Then he shrugs and turns and trudges back for more ammo towards the house, where the howls of anguish still ring down. 🐸

Djin

A MAN BUYS A WONDERFUL OLD BRASS LAMP AT A RUM-mage sale. He brings it home and plugs it in. There is a terrific explosion. When the man regains his senses he is sprawled against the foot of a bookcase, covered with plaster debris and bits of porcelain. He gropes to his feet and staggers over to the wreckage of the sofa and gapes in horror at the scorching ferocity of what happened. He turns away dumbly and looks at himself in what's left of the living room mirror. He has a black eye and his hair, singed in places, is standing on end.

He stumbles out of the living room, into the bedroom. The phone, he realizes, is ringing. It's right there on the night table. The man sits heavily and picks up the receiver and a cloud of rancid powder squirts in his face. He drops the receiver, blinded, and tumbles off the bed, hacking and gasping uncontrollably, convulsed.

Outside the apartment, a pair of tiny men in fezes and balloon pants are standing smoking a cigarette. One of them has a big spiked rope coiled over his shoulder. He looks at his watch and sighs. "So it's still the boiling water, then the closetful of toads, and then it's us," he says. ◎

Fried Clams

A YOUNG GIRL IS LECTURING HER CREWCUT BOYFRIEND.
She is leaning up against the wall of a fried clam drive-in: one leg
bent and drawn up, foot against the wall. The wind snatches at
her polka-dot skirt: short and white, with big red dots. The girl is
blonde, she is eating an ice-cream cone. The boy half-listens to
her preachy harangue, the subject and style by now quite familiar. It is late morning. The air is wild and fresh and newly warm.
The sun leaps around out on the waves of the bay. The boyfriend
watches the girl under the pretense of listening. He is realizing
how pink her lips are. He smells the warm scent of fried clams in
the air, he looks at her little ears, at her little teeth nibbling the
ice cream. The breeze surges around her skirt.

"You gorgeous little asshole!" he blurts suddenly. "I love you!"
The girl doesn't know what to say. ⑤

Texas

SOME GUYS ARE DRIVING THROUGH TEXAS. THEY'RE groggy and dazed from all the hours, the awesome monotony. On all sides, they see nothing: scrub plain, as if the earth were flat. There is a smooth line drawn in the dust under the sky. It's the horizon. They drive towards it. The engine drones. Sometimes, a small, single shape appears in the distance. They watch it as it grows, mysteriously. It reproduces. It enlarges, upwards, in creeping increments. Suddenly, it acquires detail: it becomes buildings: a city. For a few strange minutes, they're in it. The fact of scale dazzles them. They crane their necks, watching through the rear window as first the details go. They watch the shapes begin to sink, by gradual increments, all the way into the distance—until there's only the horizon, smooth, dusty, and they're back in the center of a flat world.

This is Texas. Their eyes glaze. They look at each other. They stare blankly and rub their cheeks. They have nothing to say. They see miles of scrub desert in the windows. They stare off ahead, stupefied, waiting for the next speck to appear, to start to reproduce and rise.

Way down near Galveston, a scrawny, crewcut kid in Levi's and pointed boots gets tired. The sun's high. His hands are all torn up from turning the big crank handle. He decides to sneak off and go swimming. He pulls off his clothes and jumps into the Gulf. He floats on his back, spouting water. His blisters sting. He thinks: "To hell with those guys in the car!" ⅅ

In the Meadow

I CLIMB OVER THE FENCE INTO THE MEADOW. THERE IS a crowd of bulls standing about. Women in long white dresses and sun hats and carrying parasols wander among them, chatting. I approach nervously. A woman comes over to greet me and offers me a plate of sherbet. Then she takes my arm and has me stroll with her. I glance at the bulls and see that their eyes are reddened and taut, explosive. The big rings tremble in their noses. "But isn't this terribly dangerous?" I whisper, hurriedly spooning up the last lemony mouthful. "Of course it is!" my hostess answers gaily. And turning around, she raises her parasol over her shoulder and whacks one of the huge animals right across the flanks. "For Christ's sake!" I gasp. The bull lurches away, muscles jostling in its sides, and then turns and lowers its head at us, snorting and pawing the ground. It gives out a bellow. "Get out of here!" I yell. The other bulls take up the first one's roar. The hostess is delighted. "Run, girls, run!" she laughs. I tear off towards the fence, as the bulls break. I look over my shoulder and I see the women mincing off in all directions, clutching their sun hats to their heads and shrieking in delight as the great black animals lumber and toss after them. ♪

The Surprise

MY DATE FOR THE EVENING CALLS ME TO TELL ME SHE has a big surprise waiting for me when I pick her up. This really electrifies me. She is a pretty wild customer, she must have something extra-special cooked up. I leave my sports coat and sweater in the closet and get out my zebra-striped dovetail coat, it's totally outrageous, but after that phone call I know I have the nerve to pull it off. I look in the mirror and there I am, a little kinky but definitely loaded with sexy pizzazz. I am going to bowl her over.

I dance up the stairs to her place, an exotic bunch of paper flowers in my fist, I punch the buzzer on the downbeat of the little tune I'm carrying. There's no answer, it's all part of the surprise of course, I whinny like a horse and push open the door.

"Surprise!" a voice squeaks. I look around, finally I see her, she's on the sofa. I drop the flowers, my mouth falls open. She's barely twelve inches tall! "How do you like it?" she asks. She turns herself one way then the other. "It took me all day," she says. "I'm not quite dry yet, so why don't you make yourself a drink before we go."

I have my drink, then another, I'm too much in shock to say anything. When she says she's ready I finally get my voice back and try to talk her into having dinner where we are. But she insists on going out as planned. "Or do you think this is too much for you to handle?" she inquires coyly. "Of course not!" I retort. "Why should it be?"

In the restaurant she sits on the table on an overturned cup. I have picked out the darkest, most isolated booth in the place, but even so people won't stop staring—they don't touch their food, they just lean out of their seats and crane their necks and stare. The maître d' finally has to get up on a chair and plead with everyone to ignore us.

I am so embarrassed I can hardly see straight. My date loves it.

She has me mash up her ravioli and feed it to her with a matchstick. She asks me if I still think I can handle it. "You bet I can," I tell her fiercely. I can see now exactly what her little game is. "Alright then," she smirks, "give me some wine!"

I shove the glass in front of her before I realize the effect a few sips are going to have. Immediately she gets cockeyed. She gives me a lascivious wink, licking her lips. She slides off the cup and starts doing a striptease. Horrified, I hiss at her to cut it out. She leers at me. "I thought you could take it!" she squeaks. In a panic I grab a napkin and hold it up around her. She hauls off her skirt, she's stark naked. She pitches headlong onto my plate and starts rolling around in the spaghetti.

A waiter appears at my shoulder to clear off the dishes. He stares at the heaving napkin. I grin up at him with all my teeth and shrug my shoulders. He looks at me strangely and says he will come back later.

By now my date has a piece of spaghetti worked in between her legs, she is oohing and aahing, squealing at me, What do I think now? What do I think now? People are buzzing and rising from their chairs. The waiter is on his way back with the maître d'. Frantically I throw down some money. I cram my date up in the napkin and bolt to my feet and shove her wriggling and squealing under my coat. I get ten feet towards the exit when the force of an explosion knocks me flying.

I come to in a heap under a table. My date is sprawled on her back in the middle of the floor. She is shockingly full-sized, smeared with tomato sauce and spaghetti, her ass is churning away furiously, her hands clutch at her thighs. "Come on, you little prick!" she roars. "Come on! Come on! Let's see you handle a big, fat, man-sized pussy!" ⑤

From Childhood

THERE ARE A LOT OF FORMALLY, OLD-FASHIONEDLY dressed men up in a tree. They read financial newspapers and wear bowler hats and starched collars. None of them has on his trousers. They urinate. Streams drip down through the branches, like quiet rainfall.

In the parlor my mother is setting out the tea things. They gleam. She looks out the window at the somber, cloudy afternoon, the stolid green of the trees, the crowded boughs by the hedge. "Don't say anything to your father," she murmurs gravely. She tidies back stray hairs behind her ears as she hurries to the sideboard for napkins. I see that at the back of her skirt, the hem is dark and soaking wet. ⑤

Zoology

OUT IN THE GARDEN THERE ARE NAKED WOMEN CRAWL-ing around on all fours. Little men ride them—middle-aged, oily creeps from the Levant, in cheap dark blue suits, shiny from use, and straw hats. Their revelry, their contemptuous nonchalance, disgusts me. I want to drive them off, but my companion pulls me back, back into the house.

It's a whorehouse. "Why do you submit yourself to all this?" I question her angrily, splashing Scotch into a tumbler. "I've turned to it since you dropped me," she replies bitterly. I look at her. "I'm not a *giraffe!*" I insist.

I understand what I mean to signify by this bizarre denial. So does she—but she disagrees with me! Furiously I grab an encyclopedia off a shelf and find the Giraffe entry: several giraffes are shown in nature, in a savanna. Naturally they don't look anything like me.

After this we keep apart in moody silence. I am sullen, insulted. I swallow my Scotch, clenching my jaw. Out in the garden the bastards have taken off their belts and started using them as whips. ◗

Creek

AT NIGHT VIGILANTES SURROUND THE SHACK WHERE my girlfriend and I are sleeping. I slide out of bed and go out onto the crude porch in my nightshirt, to confront them. In the oily, here-and-there light of the torches, I realize they're not vigilantes, they're women in Grecian outfits. "For God's sake!" I whisper at them, glancing back anxiously as I step down into their midst.

We hurry along a dirt lane under the trees. There's a big heady moon up. We turn off by the creek. It looks like spilled silver in the moonlight; it gives off a pale shimmer as we litter the bushes with our garments. With one of them at a time, I dive into the ice-cold waters. I come up shivering and gasping. My heart is thumping, aching, as I look back up the hill, at the shack and its dark window. ☽

Fog

IN THE FOG I GO INTO THE WRONG ROOM. LUCKILY there're no embarrassments before I realize my mistake and leave. "Whoever designed this hotel," I think, "should have his head examined."

At last I get to the proper door: I can make out that the key-tag number fits the door number. After a while of poking I get the key to go into the lock. I turn it and go inside.

The door clicks behind me. There is a girl in my bed. She puts down her newspaper and stares at me. I stare at her. "What's going on?" she says. "This is my room," I tell her. "You've made a mistake." "I have *not*," she says. "I'm afraid you have," I insist. I hold up the key and waggle it. "This matches the door number and it opens the door." There's silence. The girl looks displeased and thoughtful. "Alright, you can stay, for tonight," she says finally. "But don't try anything." "Thanks so much," I tell her sarcastically. "Let's not forget whose room this is, shall we?" I add.

I go over to the bureau. I see she's taken it over with her things. Sourly I glance at her over my shoulder but she's got the newspaper up and cigarette smoke rises from behind it. I open the French windows and step out onto the miniature terrace. More "smoke": it's impossible to see a thing. Anything visible is glistening with damp. I turn back inside. I feel grim and bushed. I go to the closet and push aside her things and take off my coat and start unbuttoning my shirt. "What are you doing?" she says. I turn around. The newspaper is down. "I'm getting ready for bed," I tell her. "Is that so?" she says, her eyes narrowing. "And just where do you intend to sleep?" "In my bed," I tell her. "Listen: I'm very tired, this is my room, my bed, I'll be damned if I'll sleep on the floor." She chews on this one for a while. Finally she says, "You try anything and you'll be sorry." Then she shifts all the way over to the very edge of the mattress. Up goes the paper.

I get my pajamas and go into the bathroom, shaking my head. When I come out, there's no change in the situation. I pause, then I stride up to the bed and lift the bedclothes on my side and get in, courteously but firmly. I settle myself with my hands under my head. The wall of newspaper rises beside me. I lie there in the shadows beyond the sphere of her lamp, and I welcome sleep as a relief from the oddball weirdness of the situation. But something holds me back from sleep, something that nags at me about the whole business. Then I realize what it is.

"So how *did* you get in?" I ask, talking into the darkness. For a long while there isn't any answer. Then behind the newspaper her voice says, "I don't know. I made a mistake." Then after a bit: "What do you expect, with this horrible fog." "Yeah, terrible, isn't it?" I agree drowsily, but either she doesn't want anything to get started or I fall asleep because I don't remember her reply. ⸙

Aquarium

A COUPLE OF GIRLS ARE LOCKED UP IN A BIG AQUAR-
ium. I try to unlock them but can't find the place where to do it.
I stand face pressed up to the dark glass wall. They don't seem to
mind their captivity. I decide they're drunk, in a lazy kind of
way—they laugh great loose cascades of bubbles and shove at
each other the way girls like to do sometimes. I fall for them. The
fishes bump into their lazy, swirling bodies, in the hazy glow of
the water, in the waving water grass. The fish flit away shyly and
come paddling up to the glass. They undulate there, staring
stupidly at me with their big, blinking fish eyes. ◑

Nursery Tale

I GET ONTO THE ROCKING HORSE. I CLING LOW ON ITS neck. It rocks out into the hallway. I look down the length of the hall. The horse turns, positioning itself. Then it tilts backwards on its curved runners, it rears and goes charging down the hall. "We don't have enough speed," I think, as through the open door the wall of the bathroom looms. I gasp, and we spring through the wall.

We sail in the night above the houses. Down below are the chimney pots and yellow-glowing curtained windows. We circle. A baby tumbles past. I look about. It's raining babies. Gently, in their diapers, sucking their thumbs, they tumble softly by, fast asleep.

I cling tighter to the horse's neck as now we bank and start to climb. The rushing wind brings tears to my eyes. The houses grow tiny. The stars get bigger and sparkling, the shimmering moon looms ahead. At its edges I can see the folds where the night is pinned to it. As we draw on, a sudden dread makes my stomach quiver. "We're not supposed to go through there," I think. "No, we mustn't try to go through." The gathered material rushes up. We crash against it. The horse struggles, it forces at the cloth, butting with its head, straining furiously. "We mustn't, we mustn't!" I cry. In the clamor and turmoil my grip comes loose. The horse goes shooting away from me, head over heels down a dark furrow. Screaming, I slide down the velvet, picking up speed. "Too fast, too fast!" I scream as I go rocketing frightfully—and then suddenly slow and drift down towards the soft roofs among the sleepy rain of babies. Just before I fall asleep, I look for the horse. I see it, wheeling relentlessly, out of control, heroic, along the turbulent rim of the stars. ∂

Far Region

A MAN COLLECTS ENOUGH WOOD TO START A FIRE. BUT the fire won't light. Perhaps the wood is wet or rotten, the man thinks. He checks it over thoroughly, turning it in his hands. It seems perfectly okay. Perplexed, anxious, the man painstakingly restacks the twigs, sticks and logs into a textbook arrangement. He strikes a match and plunges it carefully into the midst of the wood. Nothing happens. The man stares unbelievingly at the curled-up black match fossil. He has five matches left.

A couple of frantic, cursing minutes later, he has none. He feels his fright bulking gigantically in him. He knows it's his own worst enemy, and he forces himself to try to ignore it. He tells himself he has every chance of being found, of making it. But his eyes are unnaturally white and large as he paces the clearing, hands under his armpits, collar turned up. It still seems incredible what's happening. How could he have been such a fool to have come gallivanting off like this, down an unmarked, barely readable trail!

It's evening now for real. He can see his dense breath, he realizes suddenly, in the hazy chill. Up above, the first stars have a harsh, desolating glitter. The man trudges in a circle, hugging himself.

A hundred yards away, a boy in an odd vegetable and fur garment watches the man from a tree. He is expressionless, unblinking, even when, later, he can hear the man groaning. He pulls up his hood. On its rim the frost gathers, crystal by crystal, hour by hour. Shortly before dawn, he sees it's time finally to go down. 🐍

On the Lake

MY FATHER AND I ARE OUT IN A BOAT. SUDDENLY HE gives a shout. The water has been electrified.

We lie frozen in the bottom of the boat, drifting, waiting for the terrifying flashes, the ultimate, sizzling detonation.

Then my father stirs. He peers about and then sits back up. "I was mistaken," he says. "It's only the fog."

We drift, through furling and unfurling gray regions. A pale boat appears, and moves silently across our bow, as if moving past a shadowy doorway. From a great winch at its stern, a mythical fish, monstrous and golden, hangs to the water. A golden wake shimmers after it.

The yellow flickering plays over our silent, staring faces. ∌

Bones

I CAN'T SLEEP. MY PILLOW FEELS STRANGE. I OPEN IT up, it's filled with bones. They're white and look as though they come from small animals.

I find myself out in the night, on a street, carrying the white sack of bones. The moon casts dark pools of shadow by the hedges. Near one of them a girl sits. She wears a white gown and her eyes are dark and very large for her delicate face. I have the feeling there is some irrevocable sadness in her life. I sit down beside her on the grass and keep my eyes lowered with considerate, somber compassion. She shows me her hand. Two of the fingers are missing. We put the bag between us and slowly and helplessly we sift through its delicate, clinking trove. ⬧

Garden

A GIRL FROM ANOTHER COUNTRY ARRIVES TO STAY with us. She's very sweet and also obviously very lonely. I can hear her crying to herself at night. I get out of bed and stand, listening to her, but I don't know what to do.

One day when everyone is out I sneak into her room. My heart is pounding. I go over to the closet and look with trembling hands through her clothes. I go over to her immaculate bed. At its foot sits the blue wooden trunk, painted with flowers, that all of us admired on the day she arrived. After a moment of second thoughts, I lift the lid. Inside are rows of pots: softly colored little flowers grow in them. Their hues are of a delicacy I've never seen before; their scent is exquisite and unfamiliar. I close the lid, agitated strangely.

That night I lie awake, listening. I hear her. I get out of bed and go to my door and stand there. Then I go out into the dark hall, up to her door. I listen. Softly I try the handle.

She is kneeling in front of the blue box. It's open. She is barefoot, in a white nightdress. She turns her head when I call her name. Tears run down her face in the moonlight. I think she looks extraordinarily beautiful. "Are you alright?" I whisper. She looks at me, and she nods. "I'm just watering my flowers," she tells me softly. ✑

Domestic Farce

A MAN COMES HOME AND FINDS HIS WIFE IN BED WITH a squirrel. He stands in the bedroom doorway, gaping at them. The wife stares back in fright over the covers, which are drawn up over her nose. The squirrel's little head peeps out similarly beside her. The culprits look so idiotic together that the man can't help himself, he bursts out laughing. He sees the nuts strewn all over his wife's clothes on the floor and the sight makes him positively howl so he has to clutch onto the door frame to support himself. The wife and the squirrel exchange wide-eyed glances; but then they catch the bug themselves, and slowly they start to chuckle— the wife in fearful, whimpering surges, the squirrel in its high, hysterical tweeting. Soon all restraints are by the boards; the room rocks with the jangle and din of mirth going full blast.

Then abruptly the husband stops laughing. His face turns ashen. He disappears from the doorway. The wife sits up; she calls out his name. There's no answer. She darts a look of terrible concern at the squirrel and she clambers out of bed and rushes naked out the door. The squirrel twitches in the bedclothes. It hears voices, shouts, and it hops up onto the pillow, down onto the floor, grabs up an armful of nuts, leaps onto the windowsill, pauses dead still in attentive silence, and then hops onto the fire escape. At this exact instant the blade of an axe crashes down onto the window ledge. The squirrel bolts onto a nearby tree limb, spraying nuts everywhere. "You and your goddamned pets!" the man screams in the bedroom, above the caterwaul of sobbing. The squirrel races from tree to tree until it is far away down the block. It fetches up finally in some top branches to catch its breath. Its little heart pitter-patters. The wind carries up to it the scraps of agitated voices; the sunlight makes a glinting speck of the axe head in the distant window. The squirrel sits among the leaves, switching its tail back and forth. It thinks, "Where the hell does he get off calling me a 'pet'!" ⌾

42

Katzenjammer

I AM THE WEEKEND GUEST AT A HOUSE WITH THREE rambunctious brats. They race around the living room after breakfast, screaming. "Pint-sized hooligans," I mutter, making for the door. I head off down the steep bank in front of the house, towards the bay. Gaining the rocks of the narrow beach, I pause to catch my breath. I look back up at the house, at the tangle of overgrown bushes above which it sits.

Suddenly one of the kids pops out of the bushes. He comes flying towards me, hanging on to the bottom of a vine. His body is riddled with spears. He crashes down headfirst in front of me with a great clatter and starts writhing and gasping horribly. I stand over him, aghast. Suddenly he bounces up and wriggles his fingers in my face. He tears back towards the house, laughing his head off. "Lousy little trickster!" I scream. I heave a rock after him wildly.

I stalk off down the beach in a rage. "This was supposed to be a *relaxing* weekend," I seethe. "I'll be lucky to get out of here without a nervous breakdown!" I stumble along in this fashion, swearing to myself that if I ever had the misfortune to have kids, I shall immediately strangle them. "Right there in the maternity ward!" I cry, stopping in my tracks. "Right in front of the god-damn nurse!" My hands feverishly twist and grapple in the air in pantomime—until I realize I'm getting totally out of control. "Take it easy, take it easy," I tell myself, startled by my own violence. I look around sheepishly. I realize I've been walking for a long while without having paid the least attention to the scenery, which is supposed to be famous for its beauty—in fact was a big reason I was so looking forward to coming here. But those pestilential kids have ruined everything!

I seem to be near some sort of marina. A dock goes down into the water, a few small craft bob at tether. The place appears deserted as I wander up. Then I notice there is someone on one 43 of the boats. I step closer, and my eyes grow huge in my head. An absolutely unbelievable girl is stretched out on her stomach on the floor of an outboard, sunbathing. The top of her bikini is untied; the oil glistens on the sun-kissed curve of her back, on the rise and fall of her flanks. A regular dreamboat. She lifts her bare feet lazily behind her and scratches the heel of one with a brightly painted toe of the other: I take it all in, transfixed. Then she raises her honey-colored head and looks at me through large sunglasses. "Hello," she says. I gape at her idiotically. "Oh hi," I reply.

Hard as it may be to believe, this isn't the end of our conversation. In fact, it's the beginning. In fact it's the beginning of something altogether astonishing! "Say," she says, pushing a honey-colored tumble out of her line of sight, "I was just about to go out in the bay and get some sun, but it's so boring, you know—*all alone*. Wanna come along?"

"Why not?" I inquire, my entire glandular system pouring out onto the rocks around me.

So I manage to climb into the boat and she ties her bikini top together and yank-starts the engine and we go puttering out a ways and then she cuts the motor, and we drift. She turns on the transistor. At first I am reluctant to join her at her scale of undress, but finally I give in to her teasing and take off my shirt, exposing a mass of white flesh I laughingly pass off as my "lifetime supply of whale blubber, ha-ha." With her help I lather it up with oils. Then she points a finger at my trousers. "Don't be a *prude*," she insists.

What the hell! I get down to my skivvies and stretch out on a towel beside her. And for the first time in days I begin to feel alive and well. "*This* is what a weekend is supposed to be," I think: "sun hot on your back, radio crooning, a lovely stranger at your side as the current takes you where it would." Shading my eyes, chin on my arm, I look out at the sparkling waters with their distant, darting sails, at the shore with its charming cottages nesting in the woods. Then my eye happens to fall on one particular cottage, and once more a pall descends over my spirits. I brood, gnawing on my bottom lip. "I wonder what cute tricks those little savages are hatching now," I meditate darkly.

"There's something preying on your mind," the girl says, through the brown crook of an arm. "Oh, it's nothing, nothing," I assure her.

Then I roll up onto an elbow and gaze into her sunglasses. "It's just—have you ever—well have you ever—" and I can't stop myself, I blurt out the whole wretched saga, all the torments that have been visited on me—the short-sheeted bed, the soap in the toothpaste, the 3 A.M. firecrackers, the faked monstrosities. "It's going to drive me off the deep end!" I find myself braying. "*Off the deep end!*"

I realize that I'm shaking all over. The girl puts her hand out to me. "How awful for you," she says. "But you know, I have a saying: Whenever things have got you down in the dumps, the one surefire pick-me-up that always works is a good, old-fashioned *lay*. So I was going to bring it up later anyway, but wouldn't you like to do something really dirty with me? It'll make you forget all about that other, stupid stuff. I guarantee!"

The silence that follows these remarks is like the aftermath of an immense detonation.

"Pardon me?" I whisper.

An hour later, as I lie panting back on my towel, I realize how right the girl is, about what she guaranteed. Passion has carried away all my worries in a seething tide of coconut oil and sweat and assorted bodily fluids: a carnal sauna for the anguished spirit. Now I lie here utterly emptied, lightheaded, bathed in relief, in a thoughtless sense of content. All I can do is shake my head and whisper midst the balmy sky and cool, stirring waters, "Jesus, lady, you are one special kind of *angel*. . . ."

This is greeted by a giggle. I turn my head towards her, smiling. "Hey, I really mean that," I insist tenderly. This provokes more giggles. I keep on smiling, but quizzically: something odd is going on. "Hey, what's so funny?" I ask, unable to keep a slight strain of uneasiness out of my voice. She doesn't answer, she's laughing unabashedly now. Because of the sunglasses I can't tell anything about the look in her eyes. I sit up: suddenly there is a horrifying familiarity to her mirth. My stomach turns over. "What's so funny!" I shout, grabbing her arm, in a panic. She wrenches free and clambers to her feet, yucking as if she were going to split. She reaches up to her sunglasses and yanks them off. Her face comes away with them. I let out a strangled gasp. "*I'm going to tell mom and dad what you did!*" the kid shrieks, delirious with delight. He tears off shreds of breast and buttock and plunges over the side and goes paddle-wheeling towards shore.

After an obscure interval of several seconds I find myself hanging halfway out of the boat, screeching across the waves: "Come back! Come back you little—" The last phrase is quite untransliteratable, being gnashed to foaming bits in my teeth. My voice box ruptures at this point anyway.

I heave around wildly in the bottom of the boat, flopping between the gunwales, broken noises issuing from my throat. Then I manage to recall that I am in a vehicle. I throw myself at the motor, visions of my quarry being hacked into chunks under my propellor leaping through my head. I tear at the starter cord. The motor blows up in my face with a terrific explosion. I grovel about on hands and knees in the boat bottom, hacking, gasping sulphur. "*Stink bomb*—" I wheeze.

That's how the police launch finds me when it pulls alongside some time later—moaning and babbling and eating handfuls of fouled hair. Two marine corporals carry me on board. The captain comes into the cabin and eyes me disgustedly. Then all three of them shower me with toilet paper and burst out screaming with laughter. ⊅

De Maupassant

A MAN WAKES UP AND YAWNS AND GETS OUT OF BED. He feels for his slippers with his feet. His right slipper won't fit. The man looks down and sees the reason: his right foot has grown to monstrous proportions. It must have happened in his sleep. He sits on the side of the bed with his mouth hanging open.

Nothing helps to modify this gigantic appendage's unbelievable dimensions. The man takes half a dozen icy showers, and then sits on the pot frantically kneading his hands while his foot wallows in a tub of ice water. The huge toes stick up above the surface like forms of sea life. Shivering, the man begins to realize that this is the way it's going to be, he'll just have to get used to living on these new terms. But how, with such a grotesque-looking foot! The vistas of shame, of self-loathing, make his head swim.

He hauls the foot back into the bedroom and starts dressing around it. He has a special date for this afternoon—of all afternoons! With great care he at last confronts the wrapping of the foot, trying to camouflage it as best he can as something socially acceptable. Socks won't work; he ends up using a T-shirt and then a scarf. The results look wretchedly absurd and alarming. In disgust the man hobbles to the phone to call up the girl and cancel. There's no dial tone. The phone is out of order. The man hurls the receiver at the wall. He looks at his watch. She'll just be leaving now. He lets out a moan of anguish and sinks onto the bed and covers his face in his hands. The foot protrudes from the heavily scissored bottom of its trouser leg like something ugly from the zoo lashed in place there.

Half an hour later the man plods awkwardly through the doors of the bar. Luckily, it's raining, and the bar is dark. He wears his great-skirted overcoat. His heart rises into his mouth as he sees her at a table. But lucky again, her back is towards him. He forces a brave, almost livid grin and goes up behind her and then

48

launches himself rapidly into the seat opposite her, so she doesn't have time to see all of him. She gasps. His grin freezes. She wears a black, impenetrable veil over the major portion of her face. Neither of them speaks. The man stares. The veil is so large. So wide. He realizes she is sobbing; tears hang from her chin. "I tried to call you . . . I tried to call you . . ." she is blurting softly. A horrible fear builds in the man, like a flame catching. "Let me . . . please . . ." he murmurs. He reaches across the table, to lift aside the veil. But with a dreadful sob she grabs his wrist and holds it away, tossing her huge head clumsily from side to side. ᕤ

Ars Poetica

A MAN COMES IN. HE HAS A GLASS THROAT. YOU CAN
see his larynx in there: a microphone disk, a little speaker horn.
A mailman comes in with his big bag. He opens the small trans-
parent hatch in the man's throat and pushes in a couple of blue
air letters. The man begins to recite—a wonderful poem about
being jealous of the clouds; then another poem, not quite as
good, about a forbidden voyage.

"So this is how poetry is made," I think. "What are some other
ways?"

A man in a baggy checkered suit climbs down a ladder from
the ceiling. He carries a bucket. In the bucket, beautifully colored fish are swimming. They have been painted. The water
rumbles with their brightness. The man crouches and rolls his
eyes about and manipulates his hands mysteriously over the
bucket. He murmurs in a strange tongue. Nothing at all happens, but it's really quite marvelous just the same. ⋑

Horse Opera

A MAN IS AWAKENED FROM A NAP ON A MUGGY AFTER-
noon. Someone is trying to be an opera singer. The man swears
groggily and sticks his head out the window.

There is a police horse across the street. The policeman is
standing beside it, red-faced and confused, his hat in the gutter.
The horse sways its flanks and tail, and paws the ground with a
hoof and tosses its head—all this in time to the aria it is bellowing
out-of-tune with its wide-open horse's mouth.

The man blinks at this extraordinary sight. He pulls his head
in from the window and rubs his fists in his eyes and goes over
and empties the water glass over his head. Cautiously, he sticks
his head out again. The horse is still at it. The cop is nowhere to
be seen. The man hears sirens now, in the distance. The horse
seems to hear them too, because it stops for a moment and cocks
its head. Then it starts up again at an absolutely frantic pitch of
expressive fervor. It rears back on its haunches and crosses its
front hooves over its heart and squeezes its eyes shut; its great
epiglottis throbs in the depths of its throat.

The onrushing sirens quickly drown this heartfelt song. But
they don't stop the singer. The horse continues to croon its heart
out even after the patrol cars skid up and the angry blue figures
swarm out and throw ropes all over it and haul it up a ramp. It
is still singing, as the big metal doors swing shut and the orange
light flashes, and the big black van goes rumbling away. ◈

51

Three-Ring Circus

I COME HOME AFTER A HARD DAY, AND GO INTO THE bathroom and find the tub filled with rutabagas. I stare at them. I yell for my girlfriend. There's no answer. I push the door open to the bedroom and get a jolt. The bedroom has been completely excavated, to the horizon, and planted with rice. A straw-hatted figure is bent at work in a distant paddy. The tiny figure straightens up and waves to me. It's my girlfriend. "Hi hon!" she yells faintly. "Come join in!" I try to grin at this. "After a beer!" I yell back. "What?" she cries. I repeat myself, but she still can't hear. Finally I just wave and nod, letting her know everything's fine, I'll be back.

I head bleakly into the kitchen. I get another shock. There's a giraffe standing at the stove, wearing an apron. The giraffe stirs something in a saucepan. "Hiya," it says throatily. It smiles. "Hello," I say. I can't think what to say next. There's an awkward pause, which I end by pointing at the fridge and then stepping towards it. "I'm not in your way, I hope," says the giraffe, squeezing itself against the stove as I reach into the fridge door behind it. "No problem," I tell it. I realize the giraffe is wearing a rayon body stocking. The stocking has a "giraffe skin" pattern.

I go out into the living room and drain off half the beer at one shot and try to get a grip on myself. I turn on the TV. It makes a hideous squeal, as if in terrific pain; then a face appears. I do a huge double-take, like a burlesque idiot. It's my own brother, on national television. "*What!*" I cry, grinning explosively. I look around for someone to share in my rampant family pride, but there's no one. On camera my brother clears his throat and smirks. Then he proceeds to unload the most vile and preposterous lies about me, without so much as batting an eye. ⬩

Origins

I GO DOWNSTAIRS TO MEET MY FATHER FOR LUNCH. AN elderly Oriental gentleman steps out from behind the mailboxes. "I'm your real father," he says.

We go back upstairs. He uses an elegant cane, a slim black implement with a silver pommel. I can't help admire it. When we're seated in my main room, sipping tea, he launches into the story of his life, and thereby the so-called unveiling of my true origins. I listen sourly, one eyebrow cocked. Finally it's too much, I say: "But look, to be perfectly blunt about it, how do you reconcile the obvious 'physiognomic' discrepancy between us?" He looks at me intently, and then he shrugs. He grins, sadly, and gets to his feet. "Well, I guess you've seen through my story," he says. "Thank you for the tea, anyway."

I see him out. I come back into the room and stand there abstractedly at the table, hands in my pockets, trying to make head or tail of what has just transpired. The clock chimes the hour. The door of the big closet opens and my father creeps halfway out. He looks about with great agitation. "The cane!" he whispers fiercely. "Did he leave the cane?" I stare at him, dumbfounded. "For God's sake," he cries, "are you deaf?"

He comes out a step, peering. Then he gives a gasp and lunges over to the couch and pulls out something that was pressed into the angle of the cushions: the glossy black shaft of the cane. Averting his head from it, he scurries back to the closet and flings the cane into the back and starts piling coats and suitcases and kicking shoes and tennis balls on top of it. "Help me!" he yells.

When finally we have buried the cane to his liking, we come back to the table and he flops into a chair. He mops at the floods of sweat on his brow. "An old suitor of your mother," he says, panting. Then he leans forward and raises a finger at me with stern urgency. "Now listen, my boy," he says. "You're old enough to understand certain things I'm going to tell you." I look   5 3 back into those bulging, green and gray eyes of his, and despite myself I feel my knees getting weak. "That thing in there—you've got to keep it hidden. Whatever happens, *never let your mother see it!*" He seizes hold of one of my wrists. "Do you understand me?" he cries. ✑

Honky-Tonk

A GIRL FALLS DOWN AND BREAKS HER NECK. THE AN-
gel sent to accompany her spirit to the afterlife falls in love with
her. Instead of processing her, he breaks his heavenly vows and
gives her back her life. Then he loses his head completely and
runs off with her.

The two of them set up housekeeping in a trailer court on the
edge of town. To make ends meet the angel does carpentry work
around the place. At lunchtime the girl is waiting for him back
in the trailer, decked out in mail-order intimate fluff. The angel
barely has time to get off the corset that hides his wings before the
two of them are going at it madly between the sheets. The TV
glares steadily over the little sink.

At first the angel's deep-seated delicacy is appalled by the
world he finds himself in. But in a while his pristine exquisiteness coarsens; the booze and the lust and the slapdash diet
make him bloated, and sometimes he curses without giving it
a second thought. The girl gets bored hanging out all the time
in the trailer, so the two of them start going out to honky-tonks
all evening, and then most of the night. The angel is allergic
to the smoke. One of his eyes swells up peculiarly; blotches
break out on his skin. Perhaps it's because of these broken-
down looks that one night the girl goes out to the bathroom,
and keeps going, out the back door. Her hurrying heels crackle
on the gravel. There's a pickup truck waiting under the moon
with its motor running; there's a tall figure in a ten-gallon hat
at the wheel.

The angel stays on alone in the trailer court with his heart-
ache. But mostly he's sinking down in the bars. His fumbled
quarters find the saddest songs on the jukebox; his tears and
whiskey spill over the selection buttons as he cries along. Or he
raises his beautiful angel's voice and gurgles along up into the
smoke. One forgotten afternoon he hocks his angel's wings for

more drinking money. Then he's nothing better than one more poor lush with a fancy past.

And these last words are the first words of the very first song he comes to write one midnight of his desolation. He writes more like them, then better than them, and he sings them and one day a passing someone hears them and is struck as if by a revelation. And then another whole story begins, and music is the angel's salvation. 🕭

Soup Bone

A MAN JUMPS OUT OF AN AIRPLANE. SOBBING, HE EMP-
ties a shoe box of love letters into the whooshing air. The letters
shoot up and stick against the puffy bottoms of some clouds. The
man looks, and groans unhappily, but then gets caught back up
in the tumult of falling. He gulps and clutches at his head but his
hat is long since gone. A cloud rushes up under his feet and the
man cringes and crashes into it. The cloud flings him up in the
air, as if it were foam rubber. He sprawls back down onto it in a
heap. It's a tiny cloud and the man clings to it, desperately, like
a shipwreck survivor hanging on to the side of a barrel.

He looks around. Out of nowhere, something hits right next to
him and bounces away into the sky: it's a big soup bone, the kind
dogs love. The man looks up and sees the looming, onrushing
image of a dalmation hurtling towards him. The dog barks and
flails as if skidding on vertical ice. Its tongue trails up over its
nose, its ears stream straight up. The man gives a shout and
frantically flaps his feet to try to maneuver out of the way. The
dog crashes right on top of him. The cloud heaves violently. The
man almost loses his grip. The dog scrambles and slides down the
man's leg and hangs on to an ankle. "Let go, let go," the man
shouts at it. He kicks furiously with the leg but the dog hangs on
for dear life, whining, eyes shut tight. "You dumb mutt, let go!"
the man screams. He feels his aching fingers slipping. He gives a
terrific leg shake and then frantically lets go with one hand to
deliver a wild, desperate punch. He misses. The cloud capsizes
and pops loose. Screaming and whining and barking, the man
and the dog tumble headlong into the wide blue sky. ◑

Strawberries

I'M IN BED WITH A GIRL WHOSE FACE, IN THE DARK-ness, is covered with strange-looking bumps. When we start nuz-zling, my nostrils fill with something sweet, something heavenly. Tentatively I put my tongue onto one of the bumps. I nibble. My palate swoons. Feverishly I start munching.

"Stop it!" she cries. She shoves me away, hard. She thrashes to a sitting position. "I knew it," she says, "you're only interested in me for my damn strawberries!" "Of course not," I protest, trying to look sincerely shocked. "How can you say that! It's merely I've never experienced anything like this—and they are, well, frankly, you know, delicious, my favorite fruit, that's all. Honestly." "It's what they all say," she snorts. "Look, enough nibbling. How's about the real thing, huh?" "Of course!" I say. "Just one more teensy snack for energy—" "No!" she roars, twisting her head away and smacking her fist into the quilt. "Sex or nothing!" "Okay, okay," I tell her. "No need to get all worked up."

So I climb aboard and start up. But it's hard to keep your mind on its proper business, what with your nose pressed against her jaw, where it is teased with the most delicious fruity essences. "Look, I'm really sorry," I finally have to say, climbing off and stretching limply by her side. "I can't understand it, for some reason—" She bursts into quiet, terrible sobs. "Oh God, I wish I were dead," she moans, burying her cheeks in the pillows. I lean over her, feeling heartsore and stricken and ashamed. Ob-viously this all touches some awful central problem of her life, some rotting prop under her self-image, and I've simply gone gorging my way into it. She's clearly extraordinarily sensitive, and I've shown no consideration whatsoever, just typical, thoughtless egoism. "Please, listen to me, it's my fault," I whis-per. "I'm a real jerk, an A-1 prick. You're gorgeous and sexy as anything, you know you are, to hell with the strawberries, they mean nothing to me, nothing! Not a thing!"

But even as I caress and stroke her, even as I plead with her to be assured, even as I excoriate myself for my selfishness, my heedlessness, my brutality, the aromas work away at my fuddled brain. Helplessly, my mouth starts to creep down; helplessly I feel it surround and nip and start to chew; helpless and choking I swallow, in an agony of deliciousness and remorse, as she weeps and twists around under me, inconsolable. ⟆

Little Fire

IT'S SNOWING IN THE LIVING ROOM. THE TINY FLAKES dance about, as if precipitated from all directions. They make for a strange, enchanting dislocation—an indoor landscape. "Boy, isn't this something?" I exclaim to my father, who silently occupies his armchair away from the fire. The casement window is open; through the fluttering curtains I can see a section of whitening landscape, like a picture: the charcoal-colored river, the long, snow-capped wharves on the opposite shore, the gray, sprinkling sky.

Inside, the little fire sizzles and crackles in its grate. I rake another chestnut free from the glow and pry the husk open in my mittens and blow on the steaming nutmeat, to cool it for my mouth. I hear my mother's boots on the carpet behind me. I look back at her. "How is he?" she asks, rhetorically, pulling back the hood of her parka. She bends over my father and adjusts the scarf about his crystalline shoulders and twists his drooping carrot nose back upright in his perpetually smiling face. Then she kneels laboriously to wipe up the puddle around his chair, where he'd melted over the past hour. I watch her in silence, my mouth full of the luxurious nut. She gets slowly back to her feet, in stages. She lets out a long, weary sigh. Standing beside my father's rotund, happy form, she stares out glumly through the window. "Two more years," she muses. "Then the spell will be over and we can shut that horrible little window." ⟡

Moon and Ladder

IT'S NIGHT. THE MOON IS OUT. A MAN IN A TOP HAT sneaks along a street carrying a bouquet of flowers and a ladder. The ladder is painted white. The shadows in the street are black as ink. At the silhouette of a house, the man stops. With exaggerated, stylized movements, he looks up the street then down the street, his face framed by the rungs of the ladder. The street is empty. The man props the ladder against the side of the house, under an open window with a flowerpot. The side of the house sways a bit. The man starts up the ladder, all elbows and flowers, in his top hat and boutonniere and balloon trousers.

On the roof of the house next door, the painted silhouette of a cat glides out creaking from behind a chimney. Its mouth opens and closes and emits a "miaow, miaow" sound. Its long black tail twitches, stiff and metronomic, in front of the huge moon. ᕱ

From a Book of Hours

BESIDE A STREAM A MAN IS READING. HE SITS AGAINST a tree, one knee drawn up as support for his book. Next to him a long slender pole is propped; a line dangles into the water.

The open pages of the book show an illustrated, gilded scene: a tiny figure by a stream, fields giving on to a town beyond. In the fields, men and women bend over curved bundles of wheat. Their scythes make dark punctuations of the harvest.

The man smiles, as if pleased with what he sees. Then he yawns and looks over at the pole. He shifts his gaze a bit and considers the prospect of the town in the distance: the familiar spires and gables. He surveys the fields, before returning to the book.

A shadowiness comes over the surrounding landscape, as if a cloud were passing in front of the sun. It is the man's hand, about to turn the page. ◗

Two Bears

A MAN RENTS TWO BEARS. ONE OF THE BEARS WEARS A little blue fez; on his vest is his name: "Bruno." The other bear wears a red fez. His vest says "Hugo." The man takes the bears home with him.

In his living room, the man pulls off his coat and frees the tails of his shirt and gets a beer from the icebox. He asks the bears what they'll have to drink, but they shake their heads. He sinks back in the armchair and lets out a long sigh and flexes his stockinged feet. After a while he leans forward with his elbows on his knees and he looks at the bears. He asks if either one of them is up for sex with him. The bears stop playing with the hoop they brought along. They glance at each other darkly under creased brows. The man pulls out his wallet. "I'll make it worth your while," he says. The bears look at the money. The bear named Hugo finally shakes his head. The other bear, Bruno, glances at Hugo. He thinks to himself, and he shrugs. He takes the money and pushes it carefully under his blue fez. He follows the man into the bedroom. He shuts the door.

The bear named Hugo stands at the fireplace. He taps the hoop up and down. Then he lets it fall. He pads over to the television. He looks at the gray, blank screen, at the row of knobs. He wanders over to the armchair. He lowers himself into it and lounges back, gingerly. He lifts the beer can and sniffs it, uncertainly, under his black olive nose. From the bedroom, he hears sounds. He hears the other bear give a sudden, snarling growl. He hears the man making hoarse, fierce noises.

The bedroom door opens. The bear scrambles out of the chair. The man comes out. He finishes adjusting the fit of his pants. He strolls by the bear, into the kitchen, snapping his fingers. The bear named Bruno shuffles out. He comes shuffling stiffly over to the fireplace. The other bear watches him. When Bruno finally raises his eyes, they are ashamed and vulnerable, ready to take offense. The two bears look at each other. There is a long pause of silence. Then suddenly the bear named Hugo starts sputtering. Bruno watches him. He pushes him in the chest. Hugo turns with the blow and hangs on to the mantelpiece with one paw and clutches his low belly with the other. He shivers and sputters with stifled laughter, his vest and red fez jiggling, his eyes squeezed shut, his hams quivering. A big, embarrassed grin spreads over Bruno's snout. He glances over his shoulder. He swats Hugo on the arm. Hugo quakes uncontrollably. Bruno looks down at the floor, grinning. Then he takes off his blue fez. He holds it cup-wise in his paws and gazes at it.

At last Hugo turns back from the mantel. He wipes his tearing eyes, shaking his head, still chuckling. He sees the fez in Bruno's paws. He looks at it. He falls silent. The two bears stand head to head, in silence, gazing at the money in the fez.

From the kitchen come the sounds of ice, liquid, whistling. ◑

Golden Years

ON THE BUS, I MEET A GUY WHO SAYS HIS HOBBY IS
jails. I go with him to his house to take a look at a cell he has
constructed. In the backyard I get a shock: there is a primitive sort
of stockade there; inside are my mother and father, looking
wretched and frightened. "What the hell's going on?" I demand.
"Do you know them?" asks the guy. "Of course I know them!" I
tell him.

I lead them down the street, away from the house. They're
very shaky, and they lean on me, walking slow. The marks of the
manacles are still on their wrists. "He seemed like such a nice
young man when we met him," says my mother. "Oh for Christ's
sake!" I burst out at her, furious at her feebleness, at my own
apprehension of the vast evil of the world. "Can't you be more
careful? Don't you understand people prey on people like you?
How could you have been so naïve!"

This excoriation produces a chastened silence. We move
along, heads bowed for our various reasons. After a while my
mother looks up and glances at my father and says, "But you
know, the food was very good." "Yes," my father agrees hurriedly, "the food was excellent, surprisingly!" But then they see
the look on my face, and there's nothing further said the rest of
the way. ❧

Talk

A MAN DEVELOPS A HIGHLY SOPHISTICATED WAY OF communicating. It's a language of arcane and inspired symbols, dedicated to the art of being witty. It has exquisitely abstruse features. No one can understand the man, but that doesn't perturb him. He goes for long walks, and then sits in a scenic area of the park and tells himself cunning, subtle, utterly brilliant little jokes at which he chuckles and wipes his eyes and shakes his head, knocked out by his own genius.

One day a tubby black and white dog follows the man into the park. It watches the man settle himself onto his bench and begin murmuring his witticisms. The dog laughs and tells the man he doesn't have a bad sense of humor at all. The man sits frozen to the bench. Slowly he turns and looks at the dog. Disbelief gives way to horror. "Nobody in the whole world can understand me," he thinks, "except for this dog? How clever does that make me and my language?" The dog sits wagging its tail, looking on pleasantly. Then it grins. "You little bastard," the man hisses.

That night the man stays up until the crack of dawn, tinkering feverishly with his linguistic complex. The next afternoon, haggard, he makes his way to the park. The dog comes trotting in after him. He takes his seat on the bench. His hands are shaking. He sits on them. He looks down along his shoulder at the dog, which is seated nearby on the grass, its head cocked and uplifted in a parody of solicitous attentiveness. The man glares at it. Then he shuts his eyes and launches pell-mell into the spectacularly funny and convoluted fruits of his night's labors. He finishes, gasping. There's dead silence. The dog looks up at him blankly. Finally it says, "That's funny?" The man's head reels. He grips the bench with white knuckles. His whole career swims frenziedly before him. "You pompous little mutt, let's see you do better!" he snarls. "Okay," says the dog, and it hops onto its haunches and tosses off a series of Noel Coward–style drolleries on contemporary themes, all linguistically polished up like a batch of rare gems in a velvet box.

The look of horror turns sickly on the man's face. "Stop it, stop it!" he blurts out finally. "Those aren't funny," he adds, in a stiff, miserable voice. But it's obvious they're all killers, every one of them. For a long time the man sits staring wretchedly at the dog. The dog wags its tail quietly, looking off discreetly. Finally without a word the man rises and wobbles off slowly towards the exit of the park, his head sunk down between his shoulders. The dog gets up and follows at a distance for a ways. But then it stops; it leaves the path and goes over to a tree and raises its leg; then, smiling to itself, it trots off in another direction. ☟

Tired Magician

LATE AT NIGHT A MAGICIAN PULLS INTO A ROADSIDE diner for a pre-bed bite. He is tired and a bit on edge from money worries. He orders coffee and pie. He's the only customer in the place, but the service is slow. He gets his coffee but not his pie. Finally from his seat he aims a finger at the pie cooler and via levitation slides the door open and edges the plate out. Due to weariness, however, his concentration is off, and the plate falters and then crashes to the floor.

The little gnarled counter guy spins around at the far end of the seats. A second old face appears behind him out of a doorway. The magician feels very sheepish and stares down at his coffee.

He gets his pie. The counter guy kneels down and picks up the many scattered pieces of broken plate. When he goes for a mop, the magician leans over the counter and wags his finger back and forth through the air, thereby cleaning the floor spic and span of its mess. He does this out of injured professional vanity. The old guy reappears with the mop. He drops it and looks narrowly at the floor and then at the magician. The magician gives a casual, apologetic grin and shrugs. The old guy takes a step backwards. He lifts his hand a funny way and there is a blue-lighted detonation that knocks the magician flying out of his seat.

The second old guy comes running out of the doorway. "What the hell!" he says. "He was acting strange," the counter guy grunts. "I didn't like it, not tonight. Gimme a hand." The two of them drag the magician behind the counter. He has a dark, scorched bruise between his eyes. They cover him with aprons and then lock the door to the back. Then they pull off their masks so their little green antennae spring up free behind their ears, and they hurry out behind the diner, to set the flares for the landing. ⊅

Call of Nature

I WALK IN THE WOODS. I SEE A MAN PRESSED AGAINST a tree. His pants are at his ankles. My first thought is that he is answering the call of nature. But then I realize he is rotating his hips heatedly against the pit of a low-forked branch. Suddenly his hands grip wildly at the bark and he slumps forward. "Oh, baby," I hear him groaning. "Oh, baby, *baby* . . ."

Shocked, I hurry away from this scene. On the other side of a hill I stop and try to collect my thoughts. I remember reading somewhere about practices such as these, but coming upon them in the flesh, on an afternoon stroll, is something else again. I look around at the greenery. The glimmering agitations of the leaves begin to take on a whole new personality. I shake myself and start walking. "It's not possible, it must be the full moon," I think.

But it isn't. Two weeks later I'm hiking in different country and I come around a bend and stop in my tracks. A man lurches backwards away from the path, into the undergrowth. He looks wild-eyed, his face is flushed red. There is a violent odor of alcohol in the air, an atmosphere of debauch. A bottle of whiskey lies next to a pine seedling, which is bent to the ground in unnatural submissiveness. The man sprawls down onto his seat. He flaps awkwardly, trying to get back up and at the same time cover his fly, which bulges enormously. "I didn't know it was just a seedling," he croaks desperately, "honest, I didn't know it was just a seedling!" ❧

Horror Movie

A MAN IS LYING IN BED. A YOUNG WOMAN COMES IN and begins briskly attaching him to various machines and performing various physical procedures. At first he's confused, then he realizes he must be in a hospital, the girl is a nurse. But then he realizes she's not in white. She's in black: like a mortician. "My God, I've died in my sleep," he thinks. But then he decides there's been a terrible mistake, he can feel his heart hammering, he's not a corpse, he's alive. "I'm alive!" he cries in an emotion-strangled voice. The girl smiles back at him from a counter piled with instruments and plastic containers. "Sure you are," she whispers. "But you won't be after I'm finished with you." The man stares at her, stupefied. The girl holds up an enormous hypodermic needle and squirts out a jet of fluid. Then in one frighteningly swift, almost ritualistic motion she whirls around and plunges the needle through the sheet into the man's leg. The spasm of pain jerks the man screaming into the sitting position. His hands flounder in the air. Then a switch goes and the machines tear him to pieces. The girl backs into a corner and sinks down, giggling and drooling.

Two more people die in this gruesome fashion. Then a kind uncle writes a letter. "My dear favorite niece," it begins. "I'm afraid I've recently become an honest-to-god invalid. . . ." And the girl moves out to his isolated cottage in the country, to take care of him. ⊗

Full Moon

A COUPLE OF BORED YOUNG GIRLS SIT AROUND ON A summer evening. Their folks are out. They lounge about on the side porch, reading aloud from a dirty book they found upstairs under the sweaters in their dad's bureau. They're in their undies. Their young legs loll over the side of the swing rocker in a youthful, graceful sprawl.

High above the porch roof, the full moon, which notices everything, notices them and pumps itself dizzy sending down syrupy rays, which fall thick and golden along the curve of a young thigh, the turn of a bare ankle. The girls scratch themselves and eventually grow tired of giggling at the book. They get up and open the screen door and go into the kitchen and start making an apple-spice cake.

Down the street, under the moon and the shade trees, a deranged sex murderer—a certified monstrosity—comes wandering on the loose. He pants and gasps, dragging his maimed foot behind him, its toes lost to the prison-hospital dogs. His skulking back is all matted hair and blood, from the guards' whips; his enormous arms are scabbed with crude, self-inflicted tattoos. He moves from tree to tree with an aimless, tormented urgency, clenching and unclenching his horrifying hands.

At the tree across from the girls' house, the madman stops. He stares awestruck at the lighted kitchen window, where the girls, as if on display, are languorously licking the cake icing from the beaters. He moans and clutches a low bough, and elm seeds flutter down around him in a moon-gilded shimmer. The vein in his neck bulges. His huge bloodshot eyes roll up towards their unnaturally low brows. His mouth falls open and from between stump teeth a slim tendril of spit winds silvery and Art-Nouveau to the ground.

The screen door opens and slams. The girls go padding over to the swing rocker with the warm cake. The aromas float through 7 1 the moonlight, across the street to the madman under his tree. His nostrils flare grotesquely. His eyes show only white. He stammers something and then his mouth snaps shut and the blood roars in his tiny brain and an eerie, high-pitched whine rises from his throat. Trembling extraordinarily, he jerks his huge claw hands up in front of him, and springs out into the street.

Up above, the full moon, which notices everything, notices the impending catastrophe and groans. "Not this *again*," it thinks. It decides to intervene, if for no other reason than to forestall one more gross insult to its reputation. In one second it withdraws all its energies from the swing rocker and stokes itself and pivots and blasts the charging lunatic with enough golden moonlight voltage to blow up a squad of oxen. But alas, it doesn't work. ☽

Big Red Nose

POLICE SURROUND A HOUSE. A DOG RUNS OUT AND THEY open fire. The dog keeps running, pink tongue flapping, black and white tail bobbing, until it's out of sight down the street. The cops reload, shrouded in gunsmoke.

The front door bursts open and a clown rushes out: big red nose, bag pants, a rubber-bulb noisemaker squawking insanely in his hand. A hailstorm of gunfire catapults the clown straight up in the air and down onto his back, vaudeville-style.

Suddenly shots ring from the house. The whole scene erupts in gunplay. An upstairs window explodes and a life-sized dummy, crudely handmade, comes sailing out. Bullets tear it to bits before it hits the ground.

Flames shoot up from the roof. A fire engine shrieks and clangs. A bullhorn bellows. A laundry truck comes roaring down the street, guns blazing from every window. The cops fire and scatter. The truck leaps the curb and crashes into the side of the house, smashing a gaping hole in the wall. The occupants stumble out and are nailed by a spotlight in the sudden darkness. They gasp and stagger about, hands in the air. Up above the fray, a yellow ladder sticks out of the chimney, slanted at the moon. A lone figure, wounded, drags himself up the rungs. ᴅ

Sport

I'M FISHING. A GIRL GOES BY IN A RED CANOE, PAD-
dling carefully. When she has cleared me, I take my line out of
the water and recast, powerfully. The fly streams through sunlight and shade. The girl's head jerks back, her arms fling out and
the paddle goes flying and she tumbles into the water.

Immediately I know I've got a fight on my hands. She thrashes
ferociously, taking line with her. Then she dives under some
boulders and hides. A handful at a time I start taking back the
line, creeping along the bank stealthily, keeping the tip of the rod
as far out over the stream as I can to avoid snagging. But then I
step loudly on a twig and that does it: she comes roaring back out
into the midstream, towards the canoe, and I have all I can do to
keep the line going out and my hand clear so it doesn't get torn
off. When she breeches for air just before the canoe, I set myself
and slam her. We go at it tooth and nail with my rod tip bent into
the water and her mighty eruptions into sunlight—flashing yellow tank top, emerald hiking shorts—and spectacular, spraying
crashings.

At last I feel her tiring. The momentum swings in my direction. I work her in closer and closer to the bank, staggering to
keep my balance on trembling legs against a final desperation
run. Then I find the harness with one hand and I splash down
into the rocks, and with what's left of my strength, I land her.

She lies sprawled on the bank, drenched and gasping. When
I've got some breath back myself, I look her over. She's long-
legged and young, the good-looking outdoorsy type. The fly is
caught in her lower lip. I grip her by the arm and warn her, "Get
ready," and then I twist out the hook. She yelps. I push her hand
clear and dab the little red wound with peroxide. As I'm putting
the bottle away, she sits up. "That was quite a fight," I tell her
admiringly. "You from around here?" She glances up at me from
probing and tasting her injured lip. "None of your damn busi-

ness," she mutters. I purse my lips at this. I close up the tackle box with a deliberate gesture. "Hey look," I tell her. "It's a sport, see? Fair is fair: I caught you. But I happen to be a nice guy and so I'm going to return you to the water." "You are?" she says, and her eyes get big, making me realize how young she is, all the more reason to put her back. "Yes," I tell her. "But first you do have to give me one of these." I lean over and take a kiss. She gives a modest little laugh. Then we wade into the water and find her paddle for her and get her back into her red canoe, and she even comes up with a wave as she goes off somewhat shakily on her way again. ꙮ

My Father

I FIND A DOCUMENT THAT SHOWS MY FATHER WAS BORN hundreds of years ago. I bring it downstairs to my mother. When she finishes reading it she looks off to the side, chewing over a thought. "Well, no wonder . . ." she murmurs to herself. A flicker of a smile plays over her lips. "No wonder *what?*" I demand, if possible more stupefied by this comment than I already am. "Oh, nothing," she says. "Well," she says, handing the parchment back. "It's quite something, isn't it?" "Yes," I tell her, "it is."

I go up to my room and sit by the window and wait for the sight of my father coming home from work. Certain things about him now fit glaringly into place: his preference for shoes with buckles; his fondness for, and extraordinary knowledge of, sea chanties; his eccentric habit of going up to bed by the light of a candle; his continual mutterings of amazement at ordinary things like hot running water or bananas or umbrellas—even smallpox vaccinations. With a sudden start of insight I realize that all those smelly dusty wigs up in the attic aren't my mother's at all, they're his.

I hear the report of his walking staff on the sidewalk. I look down: he comes marching along, his briefcase in one hand, his staff hefted smartly in the other. My heart beats wildly. His whole manner now possesses something suddenly heroic. He has breasted the passage of the centuries. Involuntarily I start to rise to my feet. How will I approach him in his new stature, how will I behave? My mother appears on top of the porch steps below me. She says something to him, wagging her finger. He stops. She rushes down the steps and jumps into his arms and he laughs, and with one powerful arm around her and his feet planted wide he swings her about so her skirts fly up. My heart feels fit to burst at this sight and I exclaim out loud, "What a splendid figure of a man my father is!" ⤳

Renovation

THEY ARE WORKING ON THE ROAD. BIG-WHEELED YEL-
low machines strip back the paving, and underneath, in rows, lie delicate old women in housecoats. All of them have at least one of the features of my mother.

Then some workmen come up into the room where I'm sitting. They walk around me over to the wall and start prying at it with crowbars. "Got to keep at it once you've got the subconscious open," the foreman explains.

A great deal of mortar and bricks clatters to the floor. Dust billows. The men pull objects out of the wall and throw them back out of the way—tricycles, cribs, skates, furniture: all of it familiar to me from a long time ago. Peering over their shoulders I can see a scene faintly through the dust. A group of figures sit at a table: my family at a meal. It is all very pale and wobbly. The workmen reach their hands in, poke crowbars right through my father's face, through my brother's shoulder, through the back of a chair, through a bowl of potato salad. The people in the scene go on obliviously, mouthing animated silences.

"Well, that's going to be it for today," the foreman announces finally. He points to his wrist. "Quitting time—got to go home and start the weekend!" He grins and tips his hardhat and leads his crew out to the street. Their boots crunch in the rubble.

I stand at the torn opening, looking at it. It's still much too faint really; it goes in and out of its forms and I can't hear anything. The dust hurts my eyes and makes me cough. I turn away and go out of the room, shutting the door behind me so the dust won't get into the rest of the house.

I go outside and look around. The exposed roadway is covered with tarpaulin; from the edges, the multiple old women's feet stick out. Barricades have been set up to keep people away.

I walk back inside slowly with my hands in my pockets. "Well, there's not really much I can do," I think to myself. "I'll just have to wait till they come back Monday." ☽

Sheep

THERE ARE SHEEP OUTSIDE MY WINDOW ON THE SU-permarket roof. They're plump, thickly wooled. They plod about in a way that is delicate and airborne. I step carefully across to the roof. The sheep are very friendly. I hold out my hands for them to lick, as I look at the sky. The sky is full of sheep: they funnel up from the horizon like little gray and white clouds. Here, on the supermarket roof, they mill around me going "baaa-aa" complacently.

I climb back through the window. In the dining room my girlfriend is reading the paper. "They all seem to be streaming up from the southwest," I tell her, pouring myself a cup of tea. She turns the page. "That's good sheep country," she says. ∂

Angels

AN OLD, MISERABLE GUY GOES DOWN TO THE BANKS OF the river. He raises his arms to the heavens. He beseeches the angels. He calls on them to make things better for him. They show up, but their mood is ugly. They tell him he has a scrawny neck, that they're tired of guys like him. When he complains, they knock him down. They beat him with their thick fists. They roll him into the river. They walk off stolidly through the mists, not saying anything, breathing hard. Under their robes their shoulders are big and violent, under the great horns of their wings. ∮

Bomb

A MAN HAPPENS TO LOOK BEHIND HIS COUCH AND SEE a bomb. His heart freezes. He stares at the stiff black hands of the alarm clock strapped to the grease-cloth package. His ears fill with the sound of ticking. At last he is able to rouse himself from terror-hypnotized immobility. He tiptoes towards the door.

In the first scenario, he gets out in time. He runs for the police who put on strange iron and rubber suits and creep in behind the couch and daintily ensconce the bomb in a special wicker basket, where it roars like a volcanic toy, furious but harmless.

In the other scenario, the bomb goes off just as the man reaches the doorway. The roof of the house bursts open. The man is thrown into the sky. He lands upside-down in a tree. After a while, he shakes himself. He manages to grip and slide and finally tumble to the ground. He gets up and holds on to the tree trunk unsteadily. As far as he can tell, he's alright. He looks around. He's on a hill; he doesn't recognize at all what he can see of the green, silent countryside. Dazed still, tottering slightly, he starts off down through the trees, looking for a road. And that's how his great adventure begins. ☙

Evening

A GIRL SITS IN HER ROOM BY THE WINDOW, WHICH IS open to the evening. She is robed demurely in white. She smiles, sadly. On the small dustless table beside her is a thin cake of soap in a dish. Every few minutes she breaks off a piece of the soap and places it delicately in her mouth and chews. Her lips are frothed with soapy foam. It glitters like infinitesimal jewelry in the last rays of the sun.

Across the street, the youth who loves the girl hopelessly paces the terrace of the café. He smokes wretchedly, in distraction. Time and again he stops and looks up at the window at his sweetheart, and his heart breaks. The spit in his mouth turns sour and poisonous, and he covers his lips with his handkerchief and turns away.

Out back among the overgrown weeds and flowers of the garden, the father of the house finishes his business in the privy. As he wipes himself, he whistles. Then he stands over the seat and inspects what he's done. He comes out into the humid, mellow air and stands around leisurely, whistling. He snaps a couple of roses off a bush and smells them and sticks them, boutonniere fashion, into the outhouse door. Then he strolls over to another bush and shakes off a handful of blackberries and stands around eating them from his unwashed hands.

From the guest-bedroom window, his wife watches him. "Old idiot," she mutters. She sighs. Then she puts on a luxurious smile, and she rolls back into the middle of the disordered bed. Across the room the youth's best friend crouches over the bidet, splashing himself. The wife chuckles, watching him, her eyes shining. "And now we're going to get it all dirty again," she says. 𝕯

In the Ice Age

A MAN SKATES ON A FROZEN POND. THE ICE IS DARK and clear; the man glides along. Below him, the faces of a multitude stare up. The man is skating over them. He is skating over his ancestors. He can see the details of their features as he looks down, whirling along.

A creek winds off; he takes it. The skating here is marvelous, thrilling, a kind of Eden. The man follows the sheer black thread as it winds between the banks. On either side bare woods spread in perpetual winter. He draws his scarf closer. The milky bodies slip by beneath him. Mile after mile he moves along, without effort, in a trance of motion; not a sound rises from anywhere in this marvelous landscape. ❧

Hermione

A MAN FINDS A PHOTO OF A LOVELY GIRL. HE PUTS IT in a frame and stands it on the table in his living room. When he entertains, he nods toward the photo: "My new *friend*," he announces softly, smiling enigmatically, shyly. One day he places a rose in a bud vase beside the photo. Later, a lovely mother-of-pearl hairbrush. As the days go by, the trove increases piece by piece: a lace antimacassar, a scroll of antique colored paper tied with a blue ribbon, a fluted tumbler of frosted glass, a pair of red ballet slippers whose ties trail over the side of the table.

The man appears to be very happy with his creation. His friends soon realize the exact nature of the girl in the photo. But they are discreet, affectionate. "Hermione," they repeat delicately, when the man finally reveals the identity of his loved one. "What a wonderful name!"

One day the diary of Hermione appears, in marbled covers, on the table. Each day an entry is added, such as: "Today I had my hair washed. Mama was very kind, though I was cross and out of sorts because the washing is so tiresome. I have so much hair! But afterwards it was very nice indeed, sitting in the shade in the garden and eating sour apples while Mama brushed my hair and sang all sorts of little songs I love." And so forth.

When the man dies, quite young, his friends preserve the living room exactly as he left it. Through their connections they arrange to have the diary published, with a preface by a brilliant young art professor who never knew the man personally but is beguiled by him and his creation. "A delicate, primitive romantic," he writes. "An enraptured, gentle dreamer." ✑

Greenland

IT'S DEEP IN THE NIGHT. MY COUSIN IS INTOXICATED, from drugs and alcohol. It makes him very spirited in his decadent, mannered way. He leads me through the rooms of his great house, knocking back the doors with a flip of his long white hand, shouting mocking and melodramatic greetings at the inhabitants. Extraordinary sights confront me: an artificial elephant constructed from pearl and ivory and tin, a group of painted men and women in a stupor around a golden brazier, a sunken pool crowded with long-tailed birds. My cousin breezes on ahead, throwing back his oddly shaped head to let out an abandoned, drawling laugh. Somewhere, in one of the rooms, I lose his track. His laugh comes to me faintly through the wainscoting, over here, over there, somewhere in the reaches of the house. I give up finding him. The night is dying. The room is inhabited by a softly faunlike creature. She lights a long white pipe for us from a candle in a bowl. Later, as we drowse, she lifts the hem of her stained velvet skirt and shows me, by candlelight, the map of ancient Greenland inscribed on the soft inside of her thigh. ⟟

Snot

I AM SITTING ACROSS FROM A GIRL ON THE SUBWAY. She's beautiful. I watch her pick her nose. She licks what comes out on her fingertip. At the next stop she gets off and I follow her. "You know," I say, drawing beside her on the stairs, "you're very lovely, but eating what you pick from your nose does a disservice to it."

We go to my apartment to make love. Afterwards, she lolls against me. She rubs between her toes and tastes what she finds. I take her wrist sharply. "Honestly!" I tell her. "Where did you get these appalling habits?" She shrugs. She laughs, impishly. "Make some tea," she says.

I sit at the table, sipping tea, when she returns from going to the bathroom. As she picks up her mug, my gaze drifts down to her thighs under my robe. I splutter in my cup, pointing: trickles of urine make their way down. I roll my eyes and shake my head and hold up my hands helplessly.

She giggles. She takes her tea over to the bed and curls up. "Tell me again how pretty I am," she says, grinning at my consternation. She rolls a finger between her legs and sucks on it idly at the side of her lovely mouth, chuckling, as she waits for my answer. ⊅

Mask

A MAN GOES TO A PARTY WHERE EVERYONE IS WEARING masks. His eye falls on a little redhead in a tight-waisted outfit. He keeps track of her and finally starts talking with her in an archway, under a flickering taper. She seems a saucy and mischievous type—and, the man bets, passionate too. He gets the feeling he's going over with her. He asks her to dance.

The party is in a rented ancient palazzo. The dances are stylized and centuries old. Some people seem to know them but the man and the girl don't. They get into the spirit, but sometimes they miss the sequences so badly it makes them laugh. However the sight of all the masks and pomp stirs up a strange, lascivious atmosphere for the man. "It's like Venice or something," he says in the girl's ear. She grins.

After a while they go out onto the balcony. They're both sweaty; the scent from the formal gardens beyond hangs ripe and intoxicating in the air. The man feels druggedly erotic. He looks at the masked, kittenish creature at his side. "Let's go for a walk," he says.

The two of them go down wide stone stairs which look painted in the moonlight. They walk along past topiary, and hear noises and see it's people necking heavily in the shadows. They look at each other and go on, almost hurrying, further into the grass. Finally they sink down by a low, sculpted tree, just beyond the edge of the moonlight. The man pulls the girl to him and they kiss and she bites him.

He shoves her away and feels his mouth. There's a dark speck on his fingertip. The girl grins at him and lounges back luxuriously. The man seizes one of her wrists and kneads it hard in his hand. He calls her something obscene and then he moves onto her and pushes her mask up into her hair.

Later, people have gotten naked and are having a sort of orgy in the stone pool at the foot of the garden. Masked women rise head and shoulders out of the water. They try to climb out, glistening, and then they slip and shriek and splash back in. The man and the girl watch from under the tree. They have on each other's mask. The girl's barely covers the span of the man's eyes. The man's looks like an industrial helmet on the girl. They hold hands. There is a tiny scarred bump on the man's lower lip. The girl picks a blade of grass and carries its little bubble of dew back into the shadows and dabs it carefully where the damage was done. ∋

Blood

A GIRL COMES UP TO ME WITH BLOOD POURING OUT OF her nose. We staunch the flow and clean up her chin and neck. She says her female metabolism has gotten all screwy recently because of an affair she's been thinking of having. I tell her I don't really know all that much about female things: all I know is what I've heard here and there. I help her off with her blouse, which is badly stained. "Who were you thinking of having an affair with?" I ask her. "This guy . . ." she says, shrugging, and she looks at the floor. I look at her shoulders, which are rounded and pink, and at the roundnesses of her bra, which are also pink. She sees me looking and she flushes and hugs herself modestly and her nose begins to flood again. "Oh no," she says. The blood is bright, the color of cherries, and it has a delicate, almost floral smell to it. I get a towel, then another, then a third. By the time things are more or less wiped up and clean again, the girl and I are surrounded by a crimson litter of towels. My own shirt is soaked. I shake my head as I go over to the sink. "Whoever it is, I suggest you have this affair very soon," I tell her. ☙

The Cousin

I'M DOWN IN THE DRIVEWAY, HELPING MY OLD MAN clear some brush. My mother calls from the front steps: "Stephanie's here!" The old man and I look at each other. "Oh Jesus," I say. We go on up. She's sitting in the kitchen, drinking tea— Stephanie, my cousin, who killed herself two years ago. Her hair is just as long and dark and untidy as ever, but it's the disturbing whiteness of her face I notice. The old man of course grabs her, gives her a huge hug, launches pell-mell into a discussion of things. I peck her on the cheek quickly and take a chair and sit watching the conversation, feeling her clamminess clinging to my lips.

A little later we walk out into the woods. She insists on showing me her wrists, not once but twice, even though I tell her it frightens me. "So what is it like—where you are," I ask her finally in a hesitant voice. We're sitting on a log. "What's it like?" she says, and she gives me a furtive look and her upper lip quivers. "I don't know . . ." she says, and she shrugs and bites her lip, trying to suppress the giggles, thinking about what it's like. Her eyes have a wild, loony darkness in them; she just sits there, shaking with giggles, trembling with spooky, secret knowledge. She keeps it up for so long it gets really awkward, as I sit beside her, trying to grin along. I realize how absolutely little I know about her, how strange she always was. Once when she was staying with us I said something very rude and spiteful to her (about how much tea she drank), which pained me with guilt afterwards, especially after we got the news. I was going to bring it up when we came out here. But it doesn't seem appropriate now, considering the way she is. The pallor of her skin is horrifying.

We return to the house. The old man and I go back down to the driveway, to finish what we can before dinner. "How long is
she going to stay?" I ask him, dropping some branches onto the

pile of what he's cut. "As long as she wants," he says. His voice and face are grim, occupied. "Well, after dinner I'm going," I tell him. "I'll stay somewhere else, I can't stay in the same house with her. She gives me the creeps." "She's your cousin," he says, "and she's had a very unhappy life. You'll stay." "I'm going!" I tell him. "She scares the living piss out of me. How can you stand it?" He looks up at me, lifting one eyebrow, one of his withering, hanging-judge looks, so that I flinch. Then he reaches down for a sapling. "Your problem is, you're not tough," he says, quietly, scornfully, not looking up. ⟫

The Greek

I AM BRUSHING MY TEETH AT THE WASHBASIN WHEN I
notice a spear in the bathtub. I go over to it and lift it out, it's a
heavy spear with an ornate bronze tip. The tip is razor-sharp.
The thing's a deadly weapon, a fearful weapon that must take an
enormous man to wield it. I wonder to whom it belongs, but I
won't show it to my father until I've kept it for a while to admire
for my own.

I sneak back to my room with it, my toothbrush still in my
mouth. I open the door and there is a huge, muscular guy sitting
on my bed examining his feet. He has beautiful feet—all of him
is beautiful in fact, like a Greek statue. Golden hair ripples down
over his shoulders. All he has on is a kind of fancy loincloth.

He looks up, regards me vacantly for a moment, then goes
back to his feet. Right away of course I know the spear is his. A
bit awestruck, I step over the huge eight-shaped shield lying on
the floor and place the spear carefully against the wall. Other
pieces of armor are strewn over the floor: an Argive helmet with
a red brush plume, a breastplate ornamented with sinister im-
ages, a set of golden shin protectors, a stubby sword, a big tangle
of straps. I would love to handle every one of these things, but I
don't dare. I place my toothbrush on the table and wipe my lips
so I won't drip on anything.

The Greek guy finishes with his feet and lounges back, looking
sullen and preoccupied. Suddenly he heaves himself lithely to
his feet and goes to the window. He stares out moodily. I come
up behind him and see out there the swimming pool and my
father floating on his back in his blue bathing shorts. His big belly
sticks up in the air; his body is strangely congested with dark, fat
muscles.

The Greek guy swears arcanely and spits on my rug. He starts
pacing about, slamming his fist against his thigh. The room is
small, I have to dodge to keep out of his way. I am startled that

he seems to be mad at my father. He goes back to the window and rolls his bottom lip in his teeth. He growls under his breath, fiercer and fiercer. Abruptly, he turns around. His face is like a thundercloud, his icy blue eyes are smoking. He reaches for his armor.

"Oh my God!" I think. "He's actually going to fight my old man!" With a sickened stomach I watch him tying on his breastplate and fitting on his shin protectors. I keep glancing out at the pool, at my poor old man floating out there. Why has he got those sinister muscles? But whatever he's done, I'm sure he couldn't have meant any harm. I want to explain this to the Greek, I want to at least warn my father—but I am too terrified to do either. The atmosphere of violence completely numbs me.

The Greek finishes adjusting his helmet. He picks up his shield. He shouts something towards the ceiling and brandishes the shield in the air. He grabs me and plants olive-smelling kisses on both my cheeks. Then he strides out the door.

I drag myself to the window. The back door slams, the Greek goes trotting across the lawn rhythmically, like a perfect animal of prey, his huge shield almost covering him. Without breaking stride he rears back and heaves the spear. "Dad! Dad!" I squawk, spraying toothpaste all over the window. The spear goes hurtling into the pool with a great splash. My father jerks up, he bolts out of the water with a power that is horrifying to see. The Greek comes through the pool gate and delivers a terrific blow with his sword. My father blocks it with his forearm, he swings the deck chair. It clangs against the shield.

I can't bear to watch. I sink to the floor, pressing my eyes shut, hiding myself in my arms. A phrase blares through my head, over and over, like a hideous loudspeaker: "Bleeding *like a pig*! Bleeding *like a pig*! . . ." ⑤

Dummy

A MAN IS BOTHERED BY DREAMS IN WHICH HE APPEARS as a ventriloquist. "We all know what that's a symbol for," he thinks. He confides his concern to an old friend of his at the neighborhood bar. The friend listens intently, his gaze fixed on the floor between their stools. After hearing the man out, he raises his head and looks at the man. Then he smiles and assures him there's nothing at all to worry about, the man is taking everything much too melodramatically. He makes a fist with his hand and taps the man on the cheek with it. He winks. Then he excuses himself and goes off unsteadily towards the john. He's gone for a long time. Puzzled, then hurt, the man finally gets up himself and goes out to the men's room. He sticks his head in the door and his heart stops: his friend hangs by his belt from the toilet-stall doorframe. His tongue sticks out huge and purple, like an eggplant.

From that day on the man is haunted by the image of his dead friend in his dreams. Typically, that poor slob is standing in tears before a dark, looming judge. He strains helplessly to plead his case not to go to hell. But his gruesome tongue prevents him. Horrified, the man has to do the talking for him. 🌒

Lattice

I GO FISHING IN WINTER. I LOSE MY FOOTING ON A snowy bank and fall in. The cold dumbfounds me, and I remain below. It's a small stream, but very deep. The green, dark slabs of the sides go down into caves—narrow and slippery tomb entrances where the motions of the water have washed everything to smooth stone: the great slabbed walls of the boulders, the little scattered pebbles.

I paddle in place, still in my fly-tufted fisherman's cap and deep-woods parka, the pockets of which undulate about me like a lazy skirt of fins. My boots plunge and rise ponderously below me, up and down, ineffectual. All is silence here, a corridor of darkened shale and the long pulsations of the moss-colored, somber current.

At night, I watch above me the glow of the rescuers' fires on the banks, under the snow-heavy branches. Figures move trudging along the verge of the water; suddenly they spear the current with the glaring streams of flashlights. For a moment the fiery lights crisscross around me, like an underwater lattice. But then they break apart, and veer off elsewhere.

At dawn, everything is grayness and silence. Then the ice forms overhead, and I slip down among the boulders and they never find me. ☙

Box

I LIVE IN A BOX. ON ITS CORRUGATED HORIZON I HAVE painted a girdle of trees, some plump hills, the arc of a meadow. There is a little lake, with a rowboat and a party lunching on the bank—and a pretty swimmer, far from shore, who smiles though a luxury liner, laden with flags, oddly steams in her direction. Clouds puff above the lake, casting no reflection, and a kite floats in the blue like a bow tie.

At night, the rest of the world hovers under its darkness. But I gaze up at the menagerie of my heavens: stars in the shape of tennis shoes and brooches shine there, and the smoky scarf of a galaxy blows among them. There is a little cork, with astronauts peering out: a monkey hangs from the tip of a melon-slice moon and offers the voyagers a smaller moon—a shimmering banana.

Now I smoke and dream, my hands under my head on the pillow. My gramophone tinkles softly, pouring its wine into the night.

I muse, and my soul sways up before me. "Dreamer," it complains. "Look how you waste your days shut up in here like somebody's parakeet. Mr. Good-for-nothing! I'm so tired of you. One day you'll just be swallowed up, like an ornament, like a moonbeam. Your head is full of moon-junk! . . ."

Thus my soul sways and grumbles. "Oh, to think that I belong to you. . . ."

And tenderly I reply. "Little worried potato, little radish! Don't you see, it's really a carriage we're on. Look: how we go rolling over the dusty road, and how the arms of the trees and hedges jostle us! The moon wants to come down with us. The streams want to wrap themselves in our wheels. And back there, that's our dusty wake—it's full of fireflies and jewels." ✦

Woodsmen

MEN ARE WORKING IN THE WOODS. I TAKE A SEAT ON the pine needles and watch the movements through the trees. I hear the sounds of their talking. I lie back in the coolness and shadows, covering my eyes with my arm, and let myself be lulled into a doze by the distant voices, the blurred echoes. In my dream, they're working beside me. They chat with me pleasantly as they carve from wood the roots, the boughs, the blossoms, the detailed leaves: the forest. "And soon we'll do you," they promise. ⟁

A NOTE ABOUT THE AUTHOR

BARRY YOURGRAU is the author of *Wearing Dad's Head*, a collection of stories. His short fiction has appeared in *The Paris Review, The Iowa Review, The Missouri Review, Poetry, The New York Times* and *Bomb*, and in anthologies such as *The Literary Ghost, Sudden Fiction International* and *Between C&D*. He has also written for *The New York Times Book Review, The Village Voice* and *Art in America*.

For his one-man show of his stories, Yourgrau has been fancifully described by *LA Style* as "one of the most riveting and entertaining performers of his own work since the beginning of time." He and his stories have been seen and heard on MTV, on the HA! Comedy Channel and National Public Radio, and at venues ranging from New York's Museum of Modern Art and Dance Theater Workshop to the Laugh Factory in Los Angeles. In 1989 Yourgrau made his film acting debut in director Roland Joffé's A-bomb saga, *Fatman and Little Boy*.

Barry Yourgrau was born in South Africa and came to the United States as a child. He now lives in Los Angeles and New York, and is performing and at work on a new story collection. ⊃